A Mystery-Farce In Three Acts

by Jack Sharkey

SAMUEL FRENCH

FOUNDED 1830

New York Hollywood London Toronto

SAMUELFRENCH.COM

CAST OF CHARACTERS

(In Order of Appearance)

EDGAR HOLLISTER* ..... *member of the landed gentry*

MAVIS TEMPLETON HOLLISTER ... *his very recent bride*

MRS. LOTTIE MOLLOY .... *their housekeeper*

JAMES CRANDALL .... *an inspector of police*

ABEL HOWARD* .... *a police constable*

SUSAN HOLLISTER .... *Edgar's daughter*

BARRY DRAPER .... *Susan's American fiance*

* ("Edgar" and "Abel" are played by the same performer)

TIME: The Present, early in July

PLACE: Bynewood Cottage, on a small estate just a few kilometers from Harrogate, a medium-sized town in West Riding, Yorkshire, in the north part of England

ACT ONE

SCENE ONE: about 9 p.m. on a Friday night
SCENE TWO: about 10 a.m. the following morning
SCENE THREE: that Sunday, just before noon

ACT TWO

SCENE ONE: about 4 p.m. Sunday afternoon
SCENE TWO: early evening on Sunday

ACT THREE

Shortly before midnight Sunday

3

The Murder Room

ACT ONE

SCENE 1

Curtain rises on the main room of Bynewood Cottage. It is a solidly built, cozy and comfortable sort of room. Starting from Downstage Left, we see drapes flanking a large bay window, before which is a large windowseat, hinged at the rear so that it can be used for storage. Through the window we can see a background of shrubbery during daylight hours; we can also—when the drapes are not drawn—see the approach of anyone who is about to arrive at the front door. This door, just below the Upstage Left corner of the room, is windowed on its upper portion, but the window is diamond-shaped panes of leaded and stained glass, so that callers cannot be seen by persons who answer the door until the door is opened. Against the Upstage wall above the door are an umbrella stand and coat rack. The low landing of a flight of stairs leading to the bedrooms is just Right of the coat rack; this flight is only partly seen, through a short section of stair rail, but then vanishes Upstage of the continuation of the wall, Upstage Center. There is a large portrait on the wall there, of Lydia Hollister, the late wife of EDGAR HOLLISTER, who owns the cottage. A telephone upon a pier table is just below the portrait. To the Right of the pier table is the door to the cellar, then a potted and tall-stake-supported philodendron in the Upper Right corner of the room.

5

Below this, an open archway leads to the kitchen. Below the archway, along the Right wall, is a large sideboard. The remainder of the room is divided into two general areas: A small dining area consisting of a table and three chairs just before the sideboard, and a larger living area consisting of a sofa, coffeetable, armchair and sofa-side endtable and large reading lamp atop the table, at the side near the front door. Daylight scenes in the room will be sunny and bright; night scenes have two basic lightings: FULL LIGHTS, wherein the entire room, stairway and kitchen areas are illuminated, and LAMPLIGHT, when only the sofa/armchair area are lighted by the reading lamp, and the rest of the room is in golden gloom—all things visible, but in soft focus as compared with the living area's much brighter illumination. FULL LIGHTS are controlled by either of two switches, one to the Left of the low landing, the other on the Upstage wall at the knobside of the cellar door; LAMPLIGHT is controlled by a button or chain on the lamp.

At curtain-rise, it is about nine o'clock on a Friday night. The drapes are closed before the window-seat. Only LAMPLIGHT illuminates the room.

EDGAR HOLLISTER *is standing at the Upstage end of the sideboard, holding a drink in one hand. He is a handsome man in his early 50s, his hair and mustache quite silvered in a very attractive way. He wears a striking smoking jacket—possibly of red or gold silk with black velvet cuffs and lapels—with a white silk scarf about his throat. His manner is thoughtful and just a bit grim; he is obviously waiting for something, biding his time; he barely touches his drink, just a sip or two. After a few moments, we hear a KEY in the lock of the front door. Then it opens, and* MAVIS

TEMPLETON HOLLISTER, *a strikingly beautiful woman in her mid-30s, dressed in a medium-length cocktail dress, and carrying a small hand-bag into which she is just putting her key, enters and closes the door. She does not see* EDGAR *immediately, and he does not turn his head to acknowledge her presence, though by a sort of straightening, a taller stance, we know that he is aware who has just come in. As she moves to foot of stairs, he speaks without looking at her.*

EDGAR. Hello, Mavis.

MAVIS. (*Very slightly startled, looks up from her purse, the closing of which had preoccupied her, so that she hadn't seen him.*) Edgar! Darling, I told you not to wait up for me. (*Sets purse on pier table.*)

EDGAR. (*Turns his head toward her, but otherwise remains motionless.*) Nine o'clock in the evening is hardly a long vigil. Was there some reason you thought I might have gone to bed earlier?

MAVIS. Well—you *were* having a cup of cocoa when I left—you usually drop right off after that. . . .

EDGAR. I didn't drink the cocoa.

MAVIS. But—you *always* drink your cocoa.

EDGAR. Tonight, I decided not to. (*Turns head back, staring out front, takes somber sip of drink; then:*) So I didn't.

MAVIS. I see. (*Tries to be casual, but her intensity peeks through.*) Was there—any particular reason—?

EDGAR. For what?

MAVIS. Not drinking your cocoa.

EDGAR. Suppose I should say there *were* . . . ?

MAVIS. (*Still uneasy, but getting a trifle angry.*) *Are* you saying so?

EDGAR. (*Drains drink, sets glass on sideboard, turns to her.*) What would you do if I did?

MAVIS. (*With quiet defiance.*) Say it and see.

EDGAR. (*Icily.*) All right, then. I *did.*

MAVIS. (*Narrows eyes, purses lips, then realizes that she has become fully as lost as the rest of us during this conversation, and the following speeches—until her shout—are done very fast, like a verbal ping-pong game, in sharp contrast to all the thoughtful pauses between the preceding speeches.*) Did **what?**

EDGAR. Did say it.

MAVIS. No, you didn't.

EDGAR. Are you sure?

MAVIS. Quite sure.

EDGAR. Then I *do* say it.

MAVIS. Say what?

EDGAR. That there was.

MAVIS. (*A shout of frustration.*) Was *what*?!

EDGAR. (*In an I-thought-I'd-made-it-quite-clear tone.*) A particular reason why I did not drink my eocoa!

MAVIS. Oh. That.

EDGAR. Yes. That.

MAVIS. Edgar. Darling. If—if you didn't *drink* the cocoa—what *did* you do with it?

EDGAR. Gave it to the cat.

MAVIS. *What* cat? *My* cat?

EDGAR. I say! I didn't think! That *was* your cat, wasn't it?

MAVIS. Yes, of *course* it— What do you mean, "was"?

EDGAR. I simply meant it was your cat to whom I gave the cocoa. And it was. (*Pours self another drink.*)

MAVIS. Where—where is the cat *now* . . . ?

EDGAR. I'm not certain. It went out. (*Takes sip of drink.*)

MAVIS. Out? Out where?

EDGAR. Do you know, I wondered that very thing myself, when it departed. It seemed a trifle upset after it drank the cocoa, and scratched at the door to be let out. So I let it.

MAVIS. (*Obviously relieved.*) And you haven't seen it since, I suppose.

EDGAR. As a matter of fact, I have. I followed it.

MAVIS. What, followed a cat? In the dark of the night? How?

EDGAR. By the headlamp.

MAVIS. What headlamp?

EDGAR. Of your bicycle.

MAVIS. *You* rode *my* bicycle? Edgar, that is a lady's model; what will people think?

EDGAR. Oh, no one saw me, I'm sure. A running cat seldom uses the main roads.

MAVIS. But why should you do such a thing? A man of your age and social position, riding a lady's bicycle down alleys and over lawns—!

EDGAR. It occurred to me that the cat, if it were feeling unwell, would turn to someone for help—probably to its mistress. I had the instinctive notion that, wherever you were, it would find you.

MAVIS. What do you mean, wherever I were! I told you where I was going tonight. There was a fund-raising meeting at the church.

EDGAR. Did you—enjoy the meeting?

MAVIS. (*Strangely ill-at-ease.*) Well—I—I suppose so. That is, as much as anyone can *ever* enjoy one of those tiresome events.

EDGAR. Who was *there?*

MAVIS. Edgar, I will not be questioned in this manner! One would think you were a barrister and I were a hostile witness! Now, if you will excuse me, I am very tired, and going to bed! (*Turns Upstage, moves angrily onto lower landing.*) Good night!

EDGAR. (*Facing out front.*) Mavis—

MAVIS. (*Still facing rear wall.*) *Well?*

EDGAR. Not two minutes after you left here, the Reverend Smithers rang me up.

MAVIS. . . . *Oh* . . . ?

EDGAR. He was sorry to tell me the meeting had been canceled.

MAVIS. (*Slumps, finally turns to face him, from landing.*) I—I was going to tell you about that—but I was just so upset—about the cat, I mean—that it quite slipped my mind, that's all!

EDGAR. I see.

MAVIS. (*Moves angrily Downstage to position just above sofa.*) Oh, don't be so bloody superior! What *is* this fox-and-hounds game you've been playing since I got back here?! What are you accusing me of?!

EDGAR. (*Quietly takes sip of drink; then:*) Do you know where I finally lost track of the cat? Sudbury Lane.

MAVIS. (*Her eyes widen fractionally, and a hand goes to her throat.*) Sudbury Lane? How—how strange! Why in the world would the cat go to Sudbury Lane?

EDGAR. I thought he might be trying to find—you.

MAVIS. Preposterous.

EDGAR. You were nowhere near Sudbury Lane tonight?

MAVIS. Well—I—I *may* have been. Afte. all, it *is* between here and the church. I may have driven along it—I'm sure I don't remember.

EDGAR. (*Finishes drink; then:*) Then you don't remember parking the car there? (*Quietly pours himself another drink.*)

MAVIS. (*Her mind working desperately, hesitates; then:*) Oh, of course! How silly of me! Yes, I *did* park for awhile! I just didn't realize it was on Sudbury Lane, that's all. I—I had a beastly headache. I thought a short stroll in the open air would help it.

EDGAR. But you weren't *in* the open air, my dear. You were in the second-floor flat of the building in front of which you had parked.

MAVIS. What? But—really— Oh, of course! Yes, now I remember!

EDGAR. Remember what?

MAVIS. I had a packet of headache powders with me, but I needed a glass of water to take them with. I saw a light in the window of the flat, so I ran upstairs and simply asked the nice little old lady who lives there for a glass of water.

EDGAR. Little old lady? In the second-floor flat on Sudbury Lane?

MAVIS. Why *shouldn't* there be a little old lady in the second-floor flat on Sudbury Lane?

EDGAR. Because there was a man's name on the bell-push in the downstairs hall.

MAVIS. A man's name?

EDGAR. On the bell-push.

MAVIS. Oh, yes, of course, now I remember! The little old lady had just recently moved in, and hadn't had a chance to put her own name on the bell-push, that's all.

EDGAR. How could you possibly know that?

MAVIS. She told me. While I was taking the headache powders. She—she was quite talkative.

EDGAR. I see.

MAVIS. Don't you dare say "I see" in that superior tone! I asked for water, she gave me some, and while I drank it she told me she had just moved in and hadn't had a chance to put her name upon the bell-push!

EDGAR. Then why did I hear a man's voice when I listened at the door?

MAVIS. You listened?

EDGAR. At the door.

MAVIS. That was a swinish thing to do! I had no idea you were so suspicious!

EDGAR. Mavis, I was not suspicious, merely curious. And I did hear a man's voice in the flat.

MAVIS. It was the radio, you silly fool! Little old ladies often keep the radio on, day and night, for companionship!

EDGAR. And then I heard a champagne cork pop!

MAVIS. That was the little old lady's knee! She has arthritis. It pops all the time, she said.

EDGAR. I only heard it pop once.

MAVIS. She only flexed it once.

EDGAR. And I heard you laughing.

MAVIS. Naturally. She looked very silly when she popped her knee.

EDGAR. And rumba music!

MAVIS. She put on a recording. She does the rumba to exercise her stiff knee. It's some sort of therapy.

EDGAR. Then why didn't it pop again?

MAVIS. Because the therapy is working, of course!

EDGAR. But I distinctly heard your voice say "Darling"!

MAVIS. She was a darling old lady!

EDGAR. And you laughed again!

MAVIS. Her rumba is ludicrous!

EDGAR. And the clink of glasses!

MAVIS. I was finished with my water!

EDGAR. Then you gave a whoop of glee!

MAVIS. Edgar, I never whoop! That was her schnauzer. I had trodden upon the poor creature's tail, that's all.

EDGAR. (*About to sip drink, pauses, blinks in puzzlement.*) I say, darling—is this true?

MAVIS. But of *course* it is, my dearest! Why? What did you *think* was the truth?

EDGAR. (*Stares floorward, ashamed.*) I hardly dare tell you. I'm so overcome with remorse to have ever for a moment doubted you!

MAVIS. (*Smiles with feigned warmth and genuine relief.*) Nonsense, darling, anyone might have imagined things under the circumstances.

EDGAR. (*Sets drink down, turns to her.*) Mavis, my darling, can you ever forgive me?

MAVIS. (*Holds out her arms.*) Of course I can! I'm so sorry I worried you! What an unpleasant evening you must have spent!

EDGAR. (*Goes to her, embraces her, pillows cheek upon her shoulder.*) I've been an utter fool!

MAVIS. (*Stroking his hair gently, but—unseen by him—smiling in cold and quite chilling triumph.*) Now-now . . . !

EDGAR. But I have!

MAVIS. No-no . . . !

EDGAR. I do love you so!

MAVIS. Yes-yes . . . !

EDGAR. I don't deserve you!

MAVIS. There-there . . . !

EDGAR. (*Abruptly straightens, releasing her.*) Oh, my dearest! I shall have to telephone my solicitor at once!

MAVIS. Sir Charles Rumley? Whatever for?

EDGAR. Well—when I came home here—I was so upset—so seething with rage for the supposed things I imagined you had done—I was going to—that is—

MAVIS. Edgar, what are you trying to tell me . . . ?

EDGAR. Darling, I've done a dreadful thing. . . .

MAVIS. (*An icy edge to her tone.*) . . . What?

EDGAR. (*Turns from her, uncomfortable.*) I phoned Sir Charles and told him I intended to change the terms of my will.

MAVIS. (*Quivering with fury, bites off each word.*) You . . . did . . . what?!

EDGAR. (*Turns back to her, contrite.*) Now, my dearest, you needn't fret. I told him no more than *just* that. I never said a word against *you*, never indicated even in the slightest the alteration of bequests. I merely said I wished to change it, but gave no specifics.

MAVIS. Well—I must admit—that *is* a relief. I shouldn't like Sir Charles to *ever* think that I would— that is, to hear that *you* thought that I would—well— *you* know.

EDGAR. I'll disabuse him of the notion at once, before he even *wonders* why I— (*Reaches for phone, stops, snaps fingers.*) Oh, drat! I forgot! He was just going out when I rang him up. He won't be home for hours.

MAVIS. Don't worry, darling, I'm sure tomorrow morning will be time enough. Finish your drink and let's go to bed.

EDGAR. (*Starts back toward sideboard.*) Yes, of

course, at once. (*Lifts drink; then, back to her, frowns, does not sip.*) Darling—something just crossed my mind—

MAVIS. (*Remains where she was, just above sofa.*) . . . Yes . . . ?

EDGAR. (*Still not facing her.*) You say you drove to church—found out there was to be no meeting after all—then started driving home—had this headache—stopped the car on Sudbury Lane—went up to the second-floor flat—borrowed a glass of water—took the headache powders—came down—and came straight-away home?

MAVIS. Yes, Yes, that's it, exactly. That's what I did. Precisely.

EDGAR. (*Sets drink on sideboard, turns to face her.*) In that case—there is something about your story that is—decidedly—odd.

MAVIS. Odd?

EDGAR. Odd.

MAVIS. I see. And just what about my story is so bloody odd?

EDGAR. Mavis, I do wish you wouldn't use that sort of language.

MAVIS. I'll use whatever bleeding language I bloody want! Now get to the point!

EDGAR. Well—I was merely wondering, mind you—how is it that your car was parked facing *toward* the church and not *away* from it—?

MAVIS. (*Trying to follow his notion, but confused.*) What? What are you getting at?

EDGAR. Well, it's only that—it looks awfully as though you parked there on your way *to* the church, and not *from* it. Which means you never went near the church at all!

MAVIS. Don't be ridiculous, of course I did. I just mixed things up in my mind, got events in the wrong order. Headache first, *then* church, that's all.

EDGAR. Did you speak to Reverend Smithers?

MAVIS. I—well, *no*, actually. I spoke to no one. When I saw the church was dark, I naturally assumed the meeting had been canceled, and came home.

EDGAR. Strange.

MAVIS. What's so ruddy strange about it?!

EDGAR. Well, you see, my dear, the church *wasn't* dark. They were having an evening prayer service. That's the reason the meeting was canceled. Or so Smithers said.

MAVIS. It's a lie! Who are you going to believe, your own wife or that sniveling minister?!

EDGAR. I *could* have mistaken his meaning, I suppose. . . . (*Steps to phone.*) Shall I call him and ask—? (*Stops as* MAVIS *brings up a hitherto-unseen and extremely large pistol in her right hand and levels it at him.*)

MAVIS. Don't you *touch* that phone!

EDGAR. Mavis—that pistol—!

MAVIS. I suppose you're wondering why I'm pointing it at you?

EDGAR. Well, yes, that, of course—but actually, I was wondering even *more* just where you *got* it!

(*In case you are wondering, it has been hooked handily to the Upstage side of the sofa by the stage manager, from which point she retrieved it a few speeches ago and held it hidden against her unseen Upstage side until now.*)

MAVIS. I've had it all along! You simply didn't notice it!

EDGAR. A pistol that size?! I find it hard to believe!

MAVIS. (*In the tone employed by many an unhappy wife, wails:*) Y-you never notice anything—! (*He steps toward her solicitously, but stops as she brings pistol up higher, and changes her mood to brisk menace.*) No you don't!

EDGAR. Mavis—you—you wouldn't!

MAVIS. Oh, wouldn't I?

EDGAR. No, you wouldn't.

MAVIS. Would!

EDGAR. Wouldn't!

MAVIS. Would!

EDGAR. Oh, very well, have it your own way! . . . But—*why?*

MAVIS. You blasted fool! Do you mean to tell me you really *don't* know—?!

EDGAR. *Mean* to tell you? I *do* tell you! I don't *why* you would shoot me.

MAVIS. Are you *blind?* Or just incorrigibly *stupid?!*

EDGAR. Are *those* the only *choices* I get? That's hardly sporting.

MAVIS. Oh, very well, you simpleton, I'll *tell* you! I suppose I owe you that much. I *hate* you! Always *have* hated you! Every moment of our wedded life has been a *nightmare* to me! I can't *bear* your arms about me, your *lips* upon mine, the touch of your *hand!* Our life together has been the most horrid experience of my lifetime! And I won't put up with it for another minute! Not another minute, do you hear?!

EDGAR. Darling, we were *only* married this *morning* . . . !

MAVIS. I don't care! It's *already* too much! (*Brings up pistol, ready to fire.*)

EDGAR. A moment! Just a single moment!

MAVIS. Well . . . what is it?

EDGAR. May I—finish my drink—?

MAVIS. Oh . . . very well, I suppose so! (*He moves to sideboard, picks up drink, prepares to sip, and then suddenly—as if she were right beside him, and not ten feet away across the room—whirls and tosses drink upward into the air (not the glass, just what's in it), and swings a hefty right across to her jaw—except that she's nowhere near.*) What in blazes was *that* all about?

EDGAR. (*Bashful, shamefaced.*) Ah, well—I was
trying to toss the drink into your face, and then knock
you cold before you recovered from the surprise.

MAVIS. (*Patiently, as with a stupid pupil.*) Edgar,
you dunce, *that* trick won't work unless the other party
is standing *beside* you!

EDGAR. By Jove! Never thought of that! I say—
might I have another go at it?

MAVIS. (*Sighs, rolls her eyes heavenward.*) Oh,
Edgar, *really*, now—!

EDGAR. Can't blame a chap for trying.

MAVIS. No, I suppose not.

EDGAR. Well—guess there's nothing for it, then.
Cheer-o!

MAVIS. Cheer-o! (*Fires pistol; he clutches upper
arm.*) You're not dead!

EDGAR. Sorry, no. Only a flesh wound. Though I
must say, it smarts like blazes!

MAVIS. Blast! I never *was* much of a shot! Oh, well,
there's more where that came from! (*Fires again; he
clutches left thigh.*) Oh, my dear, I *am* sorry! That
must feel simply dreadful!

EDGAR. (*Helpfully.*) Perhaps if you stood a wee bit
closer—?

MAVIS. Yes, of course, why didn't *I* think of that!
(*Takes two steps closer to him, fires again.*)

EDGAR. (*Clutches heart.*) Ah! *That's* got it! Ooooh!
Aaaah! Ouch! Damn and blast! (*Sprawls backward
through archway to kitchen, with just his feet jutting
out into room.*)

MAVIS. (*Lets pistol dangle, rushes forward to stare
down at him.*) Edgar—! *Edgar*—! Oh, what have I
done! What have I *done!* (*Turns, flings pistol onto
sofa, wrings her hands.*) This is dreadful! I must have
been out of my mind! Whatever will I do?! (*Voice is
at near hysteria, then PHONE rings, she lurches to it
blindly, racked with sobs, lifts it up, then says cheer-*

fully:) *Hallo—?* . . . Darling! It's you! . . . No-no,
don't worry, it doesn't matter if I call you "darling"
or not, Edgar's gone! . . . No-no, I'm *sure* he won't be
back unexpectedly. The fact of the matter is, I've shot
him! . . . Yes, with a pistol . . . Can I *what—?* . . .
Mmmm, no, I don't think so, really . . . Well, you see,
darling, there's just no way in the world I could make
the police think it was suicide. Unfortunately, in my
enthusiasm for the project, I shot him three times . . .
Yes, three . . . Because the first two shots merely
wounded him! . . . Well, of *course* I had to do it! . . .
He knew all about *us!* . . . He was *there,* I tell you,
at your flat on Sudbury Lane! . . . Yes! . . . Not at
all, darling, don't mention it . . . Yes, but the thing
is, what am I to do *now?* . . . But I can't *possibly!*
There's not enough room in the boot of the runabout,
even if I could manage to drag him out into the driveway in the first place! . . . Well, *do* come by, then,
darling, and we'll work something out, I'm sure! . . .
Right-ho! See you then! Ta-ta! (*Hangs up, turns
once again to face corpse, wrings hands.*) Oh, Edgar,
Edgar, Edgar! *Why* did you make me *do* it? Why?
Why? (*Then, as if tiring of all this emotion, shrugs,
yawns, scratches briskly along her ribs on one side,
picks up purse and starts upstairs, humming merrily,
as lighting fades into full—*)

BLACKOUT

ACT ONE

Scene 2

*About 10 a.m. the following morning. Drapes are
open, room is sunlit and cheery, no sign of human
occupancy, not even* Edgar's *feet. After a moment,*

we see INSPECTOR JAMES CRANDALL *through the window as he approaches the front door, and then we hear the DOORBELL.*

LOTTIE. (*Off.*) Coming! I'm coming! (MRS. LOTTIE MOLLOY, *the housekeeper, enters from kitchen, crossing to front door; she is a pleasant-faced matronly woman in her mid-sixties, in a housedress and apron; when she opens the front door and we get a better look at the caller, he will be seen to be a handsome man in his mid-forties, quiet and almost stolid of manner, his face so expressionless that it might be carven out of wood, and possessed of a voice that never betrays a hint of any emotion he might be feeling; she pauses at threshold to wipe her palms on apron, then she opens door and* JAMES *steps in.*) Good morning, sir. Can I help you?

JAMES. My name is Crandall. I believe Mrs. Hollister is expecting me.

LOTTIE. Are you sure, sir? The missus didn't mention any Mister Crandall to me.

JAMES. She wouldn't know me by name. But she is expecting me. My card. (*Hands her a piece of pasteboard; she squints at it.*)

LOTTIE. Oh, it's Inspector Crandall! Oh, yes, sir, she *is* expecting you! (*Will return card, close door, direct him to armchair, during:*) She's been ever so upset, with the master not returning home last night! Please have a chair, and I'll tell her you're here. Can I get you anything—a cup of tea—?

JAMES. (*Seating himself.*) Nothing, thank you, Miss—?

LOTTIE. Molloy. Lottie Molloy. And it's "Mrs." I've been the Hollisters' housekeeper for over thirty years.

JAMES. Then perhaps you can tell me—is it usual for Mister Hollister to absent himself from home without warning?

LOTTIE. Oh, no, sir. Never, sir. He was never one to

give worry to folks. If he wasn't going to return home, he would say so. I only hope he hasn't had an accident.

JAMES. Just where was he going, last night?

LOTTIE. I'm sure I have no idea, sir. Never said a word to me, he didn't. He was still home when I went to bed.

JAMES. Ah, then, you live on the premises, Lottie—?

LOTTIE. Yes, sir. I have a bedroom just off the kitchen, in the back.

JAMES. And you didn't hear him go out?

LOTTIE. No, sir. Or hear Mrs. Hollister come in, either.

JAMES. *Mrs.* Hollister was out last night?

LOTTIE. Oh, yes, sir. I thought you knew.

JAMES. No. No, I didn't. Of course, she may have said so when she rang up the station, and it simply got left out of the report.

LOTTIE. Yes, that's probably what happened, sir.

JAMES. (*Indicates portrait.*) Is that Mrs. Hollister—?

LOTTIE. Oh, no, sir—that is to say—not the one who rang up the police. That is the *first* Mrs. Hollister. Master Edgar brought her here to Bynewood Cottage as a bride, twenty-four years ago. She died, poor soul, nearly five years ago, just after Miss Susan went off to America.

JAMES. Miss Susan?

LOTTIE. Master Edgar's only child.

JAMES. A daughter, I presume?

LOTTIE. Yes, sir.

JAMES. Why did she go to America?

LOTTIE. Well, you see, sir, her mother—that's the *first* Mrs. Hollister—was an American, and she wanted Susan to attend the same university where she had gone, before she married Master Edgar. Miss Susan only just graduated last month. A terrible shame her dear mother wasn't here to see it. Of course, if she were *here,* she *wouldn't* see it, since it happened over *there.*

JAMES. Yes, yes, of course. But you said—last month? And she's not home yet?

LOTTIE. No, but I suppose she's expected, fairly shortly, sir.

JAMES. Why do you suppose *that*, Lottie?

LOTTIE. (*Glances covertly toward stairs, then lowers voice for:*) Because I heard them arguing about it, at afternoon tea, yesterday.

JAMES. Arguing?

LOTTIE. Well—perhaps I'm putting that too strongly, sir. Let's just say they were having a difference of opinion.

JAMES. About what?

LOTTIE. About Miss Susan living here when she returned to England. Miss Templeton—excuse me, I'm still not used to her being married to the master—Mrs. Hollister was quite put out when she heard Master Edgar intended to have his child by his first wife under their roof. If you ask *me*— (*Suddenly listens, alertly, in direction of stairs.*)

JAMES. Ask you what, Lottie?

LOTTIE. (*Very formal in manner, suddenly.*) Excuse me, sir, but I think I hear the missus coming, *now.* . . . (MAVIS, *attired in an expensive morning-frock, descends stairs,* LOTTIE *purses her lips into silence,* JAMES *rises.*)

JAMES. Mrs. Hollister—?

MAVIS. (*Pauses on stairs, looks at him uncertainly.*) Yes—?

JAMES. I am Inspector Crandall, of the Harrogate Police.

MAVIS. "Inspector?" (*Descends one step, pauses again.*) I—I thought they would simply send round a *constable* . . . !

JAMES. They would, ordinarily, but—you see—your husband is a rather important man.

LOTTIE. (*Darkly.*) Or *was!*

MAVIS. Lottie!

LOTTIE. It's not *like* the master to stay away like this, Missus! I just *know* something awful's happened to him!

MAVIS. Nonsense! He's—he's probably staying away for a joke.

JAMES. A joke, you say?

MAVIS. Edgar is a terrible tease.

JAMES. Then—why did you summon the police?

LOTTIE. Yes, why?

MAVIS. Well, of course, it might *not* be a joke.

LOTTIE. Of *course* it isn't!

JAMES. Yet you say he *is* a terrible tease?

MAVIS. Yes, he is.

LOTTIE. No, he's not.

MAVIS. Is!

LOTTIE. Isn't!

MAVIS. *Really*, Mrs. Molloy!

JAMES. Come-come, which is it, was he a tease or not?

MAVIS. He was!

JAMES. Why did you say *"was"?*

MAVIS. Why did *you* say "was"?

JAMES. I didn't!

LOTTIE. Did so!

JAMES. Didn't!

LOTTIE. Did!

MAVIS. Mrs. Molloy, *please!*

LOTTIE. Well, he wasn't a tease!

JAMES. Wasn't?

LOTTIE. Isn't!

JAMES. You said "wasn't"!

LOTTIE. Didn't!

MAVIS. Did!

JAMES. Come, now, which *is* it?

LOTTIE. You mean, which *was* it!

MAVIS. Which was *what?*

JAMES. *It!*

LOTTIE. What?

MAVIS. What you said!

JAMES. When?

LOTTIE. Earlier.

MAVIS. Oh, *then!*

JAMES. Exactly!

MAVIS. Well, I'm glad we finally cleared *that* up! (*Descends rest of stairs into room, comes around right end of sofa, seats herself there;* JAMES *sits again in armchair.*) I *do* so like to keep matters clear, don't *you?*

JAMES. Quite.

LOTTIE. Will there be anything else, Missus?

MAVIS. No, Mrs. Molloy. You may go.

JAMES. Excuse me, but *I* have a few questions for Mrs. Molloy.

MAVIS. Oh, sorry.

LOTTIE. That's all right.

MAVIS. Not *you!*

LOTTIE. Oh, sorry.

JAMES. That's all right.

MAVIS. Do go on, Inspector.

JAMES. Let me see—where were we—?

LOTTIE. When?

JAMES. A moment ago.

MAVIS. Well, *I* was standing on the stairs, and—

JAMES. Not physically. Conversationally.

MAVIS. I'm not sure.

LOTTIE. Why don't we start over?

JAMES. Splendid idea.

MAVIS. Yes, indeed.

LOTTIE. Inspector, why don't *you* start?

MAVIS. Mrs. Molloy, *I* will give the orders, if you don't mind! . . . Inspector, why don't *you* start?

JAMES. Thank you. Now, Mrs. Hollister—when did you first notice your husband was missing?

MAVIS. Just before I phoned the police.

JAMES. Ah! And when, precisely, was that?

MAVIS. Just after I noticed Edgar was missing.

JAMES. Ah, yes, that agrees with the police report, precisely!

MAVIS. Well, after all, Inspector— (*Crosses her leg, exposing quite a bit of lovely knee.*) I have nothing to hide.

JAMES. Now, Lottie, you say you did not hear your master go out?

LOTTIE. No, sir, I did not.

MAVIS. (*Hastily.*) But *that* doesn't mean he *didn't* go out—!

JAMES. No-no, of course it doesn't.

LOTTIE. I was just stating the facts, Missus.

JAMES. Yes-yes, of course you were.

MAVIS. In any case, he *must* have gone out, since he's not *in!*

JAMES. You searched, of course, before ringing up the police station?

MAVIS. Oh, yes. Everywhere. Upstairs—downstairs—even the cellar.

JAMES. Why do you say "*even*" the cellar, Mrs. Hollister?

MAVIS. (*Looks ill-at-ease, hugs herself slightly, on:*) There's something—frightening about it, that's all. It's very dark, no windows or anything, all damp and cold and walled in with fieldstone, and all those corks floating there like rows of staring eyes . . . !

JAMES. Corks?

MAVIS. My husband has quite an extensive wine-storage area in the cellar. A large rack of shelves, running from wall to wall, right beneath where we are sitting.

JAMES. (*Rises.*) Might I *see* this cellar . . . ?

MAVIS. (*Smiles tightly, stands.*) If you like. Would you mind if *Lottie* showed you the way? I don't—don't like it, down there.

JAMES. As you prefer. Lottie—?

LOTTIE. It's this way, sir. (*Steps to cellar door, reaches for knob; PHONE rings.*) Oh! Maybe it's Master Edgar!

MAVIS. It *can't* be! (*Then, when they both stare at her.*) I mean—why would he ring up? Why wouldn't he simply come home? (*PHONE rings again.*)

LOTTIE. Perhaps he *can't* come home. He might have had a motor accident.

MAVIS. Impossible! (*PHONE rings again.*)

JAMES. Why do you say *that?*

MAVIS. Because he didn't have the *car.* *I* had the car. (*PHONE rings again.*)

JAMES. Really? How odd.

MAVIS. What's odd about it?

JAMES. If you had the car—and your husband is missing—how did he *leave?* (*PHONE rings again.*)

LOTTIE. Yes! I hadn't thought of that! How *did* the master leave?

MAVIS. He might have gone on foot—! (*PHONE rings again.*)

LOTTIE. A man *his* age—in the night air—on *foot—?*

JAMES. It does seem unlikely, Mrs. Hollister . . .

MAVIS. Edgar was an unlikely person. (*PHONE rings again.*) Isn't *anybody* going to *answer* that?!

LOTTIE. You're closest.

MAVIS. Now, *really,* Mrs. Molloy—! (*PHONE rings again.*)

JAMES. *I'll* get it! (*Picks up phone, speaks into it.*) Hallo! . . . No, I'm sorry, he doesn't seem to be in. Will anyone else do? . . . I? Oh—just a visitor here. Would you care to speak with *Mrs.* Hollister? . . . Oh, really, why *not?* . . . (*Listens intently, eyeing* MAVIS, *who smiles uneasily.*) I see! . . . Yes, I see! . . . That's extremely interesting, Sir Charles—! . . . (MAVIS *gasps, a hand going to her throat.*) And what exactly were the *terms* of the new will—?

LOTTIE. New *will? New* will?

JAMES. (*Still on phone.*) Oh, he didn't . . . But isn't that a bit odd? I mean, calling you in the middle of the night, and then— Of course, I understand from his wife that he was a bit of a tease, Sir Charles. . . . Oh? . . . I see. . . . Yes, thank you, awfully. . . .

Yes, I realize that a solicitor shouldn't reveal intimate details about his client, but don't worry about it, Sir Charles, I am an inspector of police, so everything you blurted out will be held in the strictest confidence! . . . Yes, not a word to anybody, I promise. . . . Ta-ta! (*Hangs up.*)

LOTTIE. What did he say?!

JAMES. (*Into half-conspiratorial huddle with her, while* MAVIS *still stands wide-eyed, hand to her throat, listening to them, but not turning her head their way.*) Well, Sir Charles says that your master rang him up last night, and—

MAVIS. Inspector! You just gave your word to keep that call in confidence! How *can* you deceive Sir Charles this way?!

JAMES. Oh, I'd never deceive Sir Charles, Mrs. Hollister. But you see, I can't be certain that the caller *was* Sir Charles. The caller may have been an imposter.

MAVIS. I think that's perfectly rotten of you. The caller believed *you* when you said you were a *policeman!*

JAMES. Of course. I *am* a policeman!

MAVIS. (*Back of wrist to brow, lurches to support herself on sofa back.*) Oh, this is madness! Madness!

LOTTIE. Never mind her, Inspector, what did Sir Charles say?

JAMES. Ah. Yes. Your master rang him up and said he was going to change his will!

LOTTIE. Aha! And in whose favor?

JAMES. Well, of course, Sir Charles had no idea. So the old will stands, as is. But Edgar Hollister did have an appointment with Sir Charles this morning, and when he did not keep it, Sir Charles naturally rang up to find out why. (*Turns to* MAVIS.) By the way, Mrs. Hollister—Sir Charles says that your husband is *not* a bit of a tease!

MAVIS. (*Straightens, says icily:*) If that *was* Sir Charles!

JAMES. Uh, yes, *that's* true enough . . .

MAVIS. And even if it *were* he, his opinion is no more than just that. After all, a husband is far more likely to be a tease to his wife than to his family solicitor.

LOTTIE. I hate to admit it, but that makes a lot of sense, Inspector.

JAMES. Yes, I'm afraid it does, Lottie. Ah, well, back to the business at hand. Will you kindly point me the way to the cellar?

LOTTIE. Certainly, Inspector. It's *this* way. (*Points directly down through floor.*)

JAMES. (*Unflappable.*) I see that you're a bit of a tease, yourself, Lottie.

LOTTIE. (*Laughs lightly.*) Can't be spit-and-polish every single moment, *I* always say. (*Through window, we catch a glimpse of* CONSTABLE ABEL HOWARD *approaching the front door.*)

MAVIS. *When* did you ever say that? You've never said that in your life!

LOTTIE. That's all *you* know!

JAMES. Now-now, ladies—ladies—! (*DOORBELL.*) Ah! We have a caller!

LOTTIE. Perhaps it's the master!

MAVIS. Nonsense!

JAMES. Why do you say "nonsense," Mrs. Hollister?

MAVIS. Edgar had a latchkey. There would be no need for him to ring the bell.

LOTTIE. I hate to admit it, but that makes a lot of sense, Inspector.

JAMES. Didn't you just *say* that?

LOTTIE. It's a handy phrase. Can't I use it more than once? (*DOORBELL.*)

MAVIS. Oh, *who* can *that* be? Who can that *be?!*

JAMES. Let's find out! (*Opens door;* ABEL—*a pleasant-faced young man in a police constable's uniform—steps into room, hands behind back.*) Constable Howard, isn't it?

ABEL. Yes, Inspector. Abel Howard, of the Harrogate constabulary. That's who I am, all right!

JAMES. Oh, dash it all! Didn't they tell you that *I* was handling this investigation?

ABEL. Yes, sir, that they did. They said you were here on a routine missing person's case.

MAVIS. My husband is *not* a routine missing person!

ABEL. Begging your pardon, Ma'am, that's not what the expression means.

JAMES. Never mind that, Constable. The point is, I'm here, so you needn't be.

ABEL. Ah, but that's where you're wrong, Inspector!

LOTTIE. What?

MAVIS. An inspector of police?

JAMES. Wrong?

ABEL. Right!

LOTTIE. Make up your mind, young man!

JAMES. Yes, Constable, explain yourself!

ABEL. It's quite simple, sir—*you* are here because of a party who was *lost*—*I* am here because of a party that was *found!*

JAMES. Found?

LOTTIE. Found who?

MAVIS. Found Edgar?

ABEL. Sorry, no. But I do believe I have found your missing—*cat!* (*On final word, whips cat out from behind back and extends it toward her; he holds it by the tail, its back toward us, its hind legs splayed out flat to left and right; Others react.*) This *is* your cat, Ma'am, is it not?

MAVIS. (*Recovering slightly.*) Well, of course, I cannot be certain—cats do tend to look much alike.

ABEL. Its name and address were dangling from the collar. Of course, animal tags *can* be *forged.* . . .

MAVIS. Well—just let me see— (*Takes cat by scruff of neck or collar, swings it up so we can see it upright and frontside, now—ABEL still retains his hold upon the tail during this—and we see that its face is wide-eyed, the eyes a bit crossed, the jaw agape, the tongue hanging out to one side, and both front paws clutching*

*its throat; it is obviously the expression of a cat who
realizes too late that it has been poisoned. [Note: for
the sake of cat-lovers' and other audience members'
sensibilities, for heaven's sake use a stuffed toy cat
for this bit; realism could be ruinous here.]*) Oh, my!
Yes! Yes, this is my cat! What happened to it? . . .
Motorcar—? (*Lets it drop to dangle by tail in* ABEL's
grip again.)

ABEL. Rather more than that, I'm afraid, Ma'am. We
have reason to believe your cat met with foul play.

LOTTIE. Oh, no!

JAMES. How so?

ABEL. A routine inspection of the animal led to the
interesting discovery that just before it perished, it had
been drinking cocoa.

JAMES. What's interesting about that?

MAVIS. Yes, lots of cats like cocoa.

ABEL. The cocoa had been adulterated with a large
dollop of potassium cyanide.

JAMES. What?!

MAVIS. You mean—?!

LOTTIE. Murder?!

ABEL. That's the way it looks. (*Extends cat to*
MAVIS *by tail.*)

MAVIS. But that's ridiculous! (*Hands cat to* JAMES
by tail.)

JAMES. Constable, are you quite sure? (*Hands cat to*
LOTTIE *by tail.*)

LOTTIE. Yes, who would want to murder a cat?
(*Opens cellar door and tosses cat through it; we hear
a THUMP, then a THUMP-THUMP, and finally an
extended continuation of THUMPS going down-down-
down for a great distance; during this, all persons on-
stage pause to listen, until there comes a far-off
CRASH, and then silence; after a pause of one
second:*) It's a very deep cellar.

MAVIS. But, surely Constable, even if it *were*
murder, the removal of a cat is hardly a capital crime.

ABEL. Just so. And yet—it seems a bit mysterious on the heels of your husband's disappearance, if you see what I mean, Ma'am—?

MAVIS. I—I'm afraid I don't follow you, Constable . . . ?

ABEL. Well, for instance, Ma'am—when you saw your husband last night, had he any plans to have a cup of cocoa that you know of?

MAVIS. No! Of course not! I'm sure he would have mentioned it! Edgar and I had no secrets from one another.

LOTTIE. Wait! Cocoa, did you say? Why, when I got up this morning, there was a pan of cocoa still on the stove!

MAVIS. (*Makes a gesture of* drat-*I*-forgot-*about-that!, and says:*) Mrs. Molloy, how dare you say such a thing! You are discharged!

LOTTIE. After more than thirty years?!

MAVIS. No, right this instant!

JAMES. Here, now, Mrs. Hollister, aren't you being a bit harsh?

MAVIS. I don't care! I want her out of this house! Out! Do you hear?!

ABEL. In just a moment, Ma'am, but first I have to ask her a question. Mrs. Molloy—what did you *do* with the cocoa on the stove?

LOTTIE. Why, I poured it down the sink, washed the pan, and put it away.

MAVIS. (*Brightens.*) Why, how very efficient of you, Mrs. Molloy! Consider yourself re-hired!

LOTTIE. Oh, thank you, Mrs. Hollister!

JAMES. Well, there's no use in looking for cyanide in a washed-up pan, I guess.

ABEL. None, I'm afraid. So—if you've no need of me, sir—I will be going.

JAMES. Matter of fact, I *could* use a hand. I have to run over to Sir Charles Rumley's office and check on the bequests in Edgar Hollister's will—

MAVIS. Oh, *must* you?! I mean, what's the point? It's not as though Edgar were *dead*, or anything. He's only mysteriously absent.

JAMES. Hmm. That's true enough. But still—I'd better know what's what in case he *does* turn up dead. Could save a lot of time, later on.

MAVIS. Oh, well, whatever you think best, Inspector.

JAMES. (*Steps to still-open front door.*) While I'm gone, Constable, would *you* be so kind as to investigate the cellar, in case Edgar Hollister is lying about the place?

LOTTIE. But there *is* a cellar. Why would he *lie* about it?

JAMES. I don't mean *lying* about it, I mean lying *about, in* it!

ABEL. (*At cellar door.*) Well, whichever he's doing, I'll toddle down and find out!

JAMES. (*Starts for front door.*) And I'm off to interrogate Sir Charles!

LOTTIE. And I'll just go to the kitchen and see about some luncheon!

MAVIS. And I shall be in my room with a beastly headache! Cheer-o! (*Starts up stairs.*)

JAMES. Cheer-o! (*Starts out front door.*)

LOTTIE. Cheer-o! (*Starts for kitchen.*)

ABEL. Cheer-o! (*Exits through cellar door; Others pause where they are, listening, as we hear precisely the same THUMP-series and CRASH, as before, from the cellar stairs; at cessation of sound, LOTTIE steps to cellar doorway and calls down.*)

LOTTIE. Mind the steps, they're slippery! (*JAMES exits out front door, MAVIS exits up stairs, and LOTTIE shuts cellar door—all actions simultaneous—and we have a:*)

BLACKOUT

ACT ONE

SCENE 3

*The following morning, Sunday, just before noon.
Room is bright and cheery. A tray containing
decanter of whisky, soda siphon and several glasses
is on sideboard. Cellar door is ajar, and far off in
cellar we can hear random TAPS and THUMPS
every so often. LOTTIE enters from kitchen, calls
down stairs:*

LOTTIE. Constable—?
ABEL. (*Off.*) Right-ho!
LOTTIE. Wouldn't you like some breakfast?
ABEL. (*Off.*) What time is it?
LOTTIE. Nearly noon. You must be absolutely
ravenous!
ABEL. (*Off.*) By Jove, you're right! I am!
LOTTIE. Well, why don't you start on up? I should
have it ready by the time you get here. If you don't
slide back.

(*Through window, we see* SUSAN HOLLISTER *and* BARRY
DRAPER *moving to front door; when we see them
more fully after their entrance, she will prove to
be a pretty thing, a creature of big-eyed and
constantly smiling innocence—possibly even
idiocy—and* BARRY *will be a tall, rugged, no-
nonsense, handsome "typical" American.*)

ABEL. (*Off.*) Right-ho! I'll watch my step! (*Just as*
LOTTIE *turns toward kitchen, DOORBELL rings; she
reverses and starts toward front door.*)
LOTTIE. Now, who in the world can that be? (*Opens
front door.*) Miss Susan! Heaven be praised, it's really
you! (*Bursts into tears, which she mops at with hem
of apron.*)

SUSAN. (*Sails in past* LOTTIE, *a small suitcase in each hand, followed by* BARRY, *with a slightly larger suitcase in each hand, and will move about the room,* BARRY, *always a pace behind her, as indicated, rattling on like a merry little chatterbox.*) Oh, Lottie, Lottie, it's so good to be home again! Barry, this is Lottie, about whom I have told you so much during our delightful voyage over. (*At portrait.*) And that's Mother, hanging on the wall. Handsome woman, don't you think? People say I take after her. Pity she couldn't be here to meet you, but, of course, that's rather difficult, since we buried her five years ago. (*At sideboard.*) My father built this sideboard with his own hands. He was always mucking about with carpentry of some sort. Used to enjoy making things with all sorts of hidden panels and secret drawers. (*Gives sideboard a bump with her hip, center drawer slides out.*) There's one, now! (*Without pausing for breath, moves down into sofa area, where she will set down suitcases and dust off her hands, during:*) I say, there's an awful draft in here! Oh, of course, we've left the front door wide open! Barry, will you be a dear? Thank you! (BARRY, *setting down suitcases next to hers, has gone to shut door, where* LOTTIE *still stands mopping at streaming eyes.*) Oh, but homecomings are so utterly delicious, aren't they! Where's Father?

LOTTIE. (*Drops apron, speaks automatically while composing herself.*) Oh, Miss Susan, I hardly know how to begin! Your father's vanished!

BARRY. (*Turns from having closed door.*) What did you say, Lettie?

LOTTIE. Lottie.

BARRY. Lottie.

LOTTIE. Miss Susan's father has vanished.

SUSAN. (*Coming around below armchair, then up, to join them.*) Vanished? But how terribly inconvenient! I was so looking forward to showing him my diploma. I worked so hard to graduate with honors, and now all my effort hardly seems worth it! What's the point of studying, if nobody's around to care?

BARRY. Darling, *I* care.

SUSAN. Yes, I daresay you do, but that's the function of a fiance, after all, so it scarcely counts.

LOTTIE. Miss Susan! "Fiance," did you say?

SUSAN. Yes, Mister Draper and I became officially engaged just three miles off Liverpool, on the afterdeck of our steamship, last night. Barry was frightfully romantic, Lottie. I wish you could have been there to hear.

BARRY. Prob'ly wouldn't've spoken my piece with a witness there, honey.

SUSAN. No, that's true, so perhaps it's just as well Lottie *wasn't* there, my dearest darling. Ah, but we're deviating from the principal topic, aren't we! "Vanished," you say? Father?

LOTTIE. So it would seem, Miss Susan. We certainly have been unable to find him. (*Looks up as* ABEL *enters from cellar.*)

SUSAN. Father! (*Rushes forward and flings her arms about him, during:*) Oh, Father, you had us so terribly worried, but now you're here, and all's well, again, and I simply *have* to introduce you to my fiance, Barry Draper, who is a charming American I met on the boat ride home!

LOTTIE. Miss Susan, that is *not* your father. That is Abel Howard, a member of the Harrogate constabulary, who has been *searching* for your father.

SUSAN. What, really? Oh, I am *ever* so sorry, but you *do* bear my father a rather striking resemblance! Can you ever forgive me?

ABEL. No trouble at all, Miss. After all, you've been away five years.

SUSAN. That's true, and I *do* have such a dreadful memory for faces, *don't* I, Barry? . . . Why, Barry, is something the matter?

BARRY. Susan, darling, would you mind very much letting *go* of the constable?

SUSAN. (*De-embraces* ABEL *with pretty haste.*) Oh, of course, how silly of me! I hope I haven't offended you, Constable?

ABEL. Not at all, Miss. These things happen.

SUSAN. (*The incident already forgotten as she turns to* LOTTIE.) I say, do you suppose Miss Templeton knows where Father is at? The last letter I had from him, she and he were getting on just splendidly, and it occurs to me that perhaps they might have gone off for a holiday.

LOTTIE. Oh, my dear! Then you don't *know?* Oh, of course you don't! You were on the boat when it happened.

BARRY. When what happened, Lettie?

LOTTIE. Lottie.

BARRY. Lottie.

SUSAN. When what happened?

LOTTIE. Oh, Miss Susan, I hardly know how to begin! Your father's remarried!

SUSAN. What?

BARRY. When?

LOTTIE. Just two days ago. Friday morning, it was.

ABEL. What, the very day he vanished?

LOTTIE. The very day. Married that morning, vanished that night.

BARRY. With or without the former Miss Templeton?

LOTTIE. Without.

BARRY. Then he can't simply be gone on his honeymoon. Not without his bride.

ABEL. Unless he's the forgetful type. Does forgetfulness run in your family?

SUSAN. I don't remember. Oh, but I say, Lottie—he'd only met this Miss Templeton when he wrote me, two weeks ago. Wasn't this marriage just a bit sudden?

LOTTIE. (*Darkly.*) A bit *too* sudden, if you ask *me*, Miss!

SUSAN. I just *did* ask you.

ABEL. (*Spots open drawer, moves to sideboard.*) Here, now, what's this—?!

BARRY. Oh, just a secret drawer.

SUSAN. Father had them all over the place.

ABEL. (*Lifting out pistol we saw in Scene One.*) And what have we here?! (*Holds it gingerly by end of handgrip.*) Any of you recognize this?

SUSAN. Why—that looks like Father's old target-shooting pistol!

ABEL. (*Sniffs at barrel.*) And recently fired, too, or I miss my guess! I wonder, now . . . (*Flips cylinder open to side, peers at back of it.*)

BARRY. What is it, Officer—?

SUSAN. Constable.

BARRY. Constable.

ABEL. From the look of the back of these cartridges, there have been just three shots fired . . .

LOTTIE. Three?

SUSAN. Shots?

BARRY. Fired?

ABEL. (*Flipping cylinder back into place.*) Yes. Doesn't it strike you all as a peculiar coincidence?

LOTTIE. You mean—a missing man—?

BARRY. A hidden pistol—?

SUSAN. And three shots fired from it?

ALL THREE. (*Shake heads in unison on:*) No, not particularly.

ABEL. Well, I daresay there's nothing to it, but if you don't mind, I'll take this down to the station and have them check it for fingerprints.

SUSAN. But it's bound to have fingerprints. Father practiced all the time.

BARRY. Darling, I think he means fingerprints *besides* your father's.

LOTTIE. But nobody ever handled that pistol except the master. Nobody.

BARRY. But if somebody *did*—it *could* mean—

SUSAN. (*Rushes into his arms.*) Oh, Barry, hold me! Hold me!

ABEL. Still and all—if somebody *did* fire this pistol the other night—I wonder why no one heard any shots?

LOTTIE. Oh, *I* heard shots.

OTHERS. What? When?

LOTTIE. Friday night, just after Miss Templeton— excuse me, Mrs. Hollister—came home.

SUSAN. She lives *here?* Father brought that woman to live *here?* In *our* house?

ABEL. Any reason he shouldn't have, Miss?

SUSAN. Oh, none at all. I just like to keep my facts straight.

ABEL. But—Lottie—if you heard shots—why didn't you *tell* somebody?

LOTTIE. I didn't know it was important. Is it?

ABEL. Not necessarily, of course, but—well, every little clue helps. How *many* shots did you hear?

LOTTIE. Three. Exactly three. No more, no less.

BARRY. But how can you be so certain it was just after Mrs. Hollister returned?

LOTTIE. (*Points Off Right.*) The driveway curves right past my bedroom window, before it comes around to the front of the house. (*Her gesture has swept from Right across Downstage area and then toward front door, during her line.*) The headlights flash into my room something fierce. (MAVIS—*attired in yet another expensive morning-frock—will appear on stairs and descend, unnoticed, during:*)

ABEL. Can you give us the exact time, Lottie?

LOTTIE. (*Looks at wristwatch.*) It's just six minutes past noon!

SUSAN. Lottie, I *think* he means the time this new Mrs. Hollister came home on *Friday night.*

MAVIS. *I* can tell you that! (*All turn to look up at*

her as she comes down into room.) It was just going on nine o'clock. (*Stops at foot of stairs to survey newcomers.*) You must be Susan.

SUSAN. You must be Mavis.

LOTTIE. This is Barry Draper.

BARRY. I'm Susan's fiancé.

MAVIS. Have you met Constable Howard?

SUSAN. We've had that pleasure, yes. I must say— I expected an older woman. Nearer Father's age.

MAVIS. I expected a younger girl. The way you looked in your photographs. (*Holds out her hands.*) In any case, Susan—welcome home!

SUSAN. (*Goes to her, takes her hands.*) Thank you, Mavis. . . . I may call you Mavis, mayn't I?

MAVIS. Oh, yes, you simply must! I do think "stepmother" has such an unpleasant sound to it, don't you?

SUSAN. Oh, yes, decidedly! (*Turns head to* BARRY.) Do you know, darling, she's charming! I had expected not to like her.

MAVIS. Not like *me*, my darling? How ridiculous! (*Gives tinkling laugh, in which all others join her; then:*)

ABEL. Well, in any case, I'll take this to the lab and have it dusted for prints. (*Starts toward door with pistol.*)

MAVIS. (*Instantly releases* SUSAN's *hands and takes pistol.*) Here, let me put it into a bag for you, Constable!

ABEL. *I* say! Dash it all, damn, and blast! You've touched it!

MAVIS. (*With bright surprise.*) Why? Oughn't I to have?

ABEL. (*Gingerly retrieves pistol with fingertips by handgrip.*) I'm afraid not, Ma'am. You see, now your fingerprints will be on it.

MAVIS. I don't understand. Why shouldn't they be?

ABEL. Well, in case this should turn out to be the weapon used to—uh—? Of course, we don't *know* that there's been foul play, but still and all— (*Sighs, starts for kitchen.*) Well, what's done is done. I'll have ballistics give it a look, just in case we need to match up the shells, later on, if foul play *has* been done.

MAVIS. Awfully sorry, Constable—!

SUSAN. Oh, don't be, Mavis. After all, you couldn't have known. But, I say, wouldn't it be funny if there *had* been foul play, and you'd done it, and there'd be no way to tell your involvement because of touching the pistol just now?! (*Gives bright laugh, in which* MAVIS *joins, while* LOTTIE *and* ABEL *exchange a significant look, and* BARRY *looks deeply thoughtful.*)

ABEL. I've parked my bicycle out back. If you'll excuse me—?

MAVIS. Oh, certainly, certainly! (*He starts out.*) Oh, by the way, Constable—? (*He pauses.*) *Did* you find anything in the cellar—?

ABEL. Yes and no, Ma'am. I did find something a bit odd, but certainly nothing that smacks of the criminal. (*Makes a sweeping gesture from foot of stairs to area directly Downstage of sofa area, as he says:*) There's a brand-new wine rack that runs from this general area over to that, down in the cellar. It quite walls off the cellar area just under the front part of this room. Tried to get a peep behind it, but it's nailed up tighter than a drum. Would you know what's behind it, ma'am?

MAVIS. No, I'm sorry, I wouldn't. But perhaps Susan would know? After all, she has lived most of her life here.

SUSAN. The front area of the cellar, you say? *Nothing*, to my knowledge. It was always damp there—the walls seeped much water after a heavy rain—so my father simply sealed it off, years and years ago.

BARRY. That would seem to explain it, Constable.

ABEL. Yes. Yes, it would certainly seem so. Well— I'm off! (*Exits through kitchen archway.*)

MAVIS. Well, now, let's all sit down and get to know one another, shall we? Lottie, would you see to some lunch? (*Leads way to sofa area, where she will sit* BARRY *on her right, leaving* SUSAN *to sit by herself in armchair.*)

LOTTIE. Yes, Mrs. Hollister! (*Exits to kitchen.*)

MAVIS. (*Pats* BARRY *a bit over-fondly on knee.*) Come now, you must tell me all about yourself. I daresay I should show some concern over who is about to marry into our family! (*Outside window, we see* JAMES *approaching front door.*)

BARRY. (*Shrugs with embarrassment.*) Oh—not much to tell—I'm just a run-of-the-mill handsome young American millionaire who fell head-over-heels in love one moonlit night with your charming step-daughter, despite the fact that I know next-to-nothing about her, or her family, or her background, or anything, but I'll be just plain hornswoggled if this little gal didn't throw me for a loop the moment she batted those pretty little eyes my way!

MAVIS. (*Has located the key word in all this tangled syntax.*) Millionaire? (*Shifts position to sit a bit closer to him; DOORBELL rings.*) Oh, would you get that, please, Susan? (*Flings an arm across back of sofa behind* BARRY, *leans closer.*)

SUSAN. Certainly, Mavis! (*Rises, hurries to front door.*)

BARRY. (*Noting arm and nearness.*) You British folks sure know how to make a Yankee feel welcome! I thought you'd be kind of cold and reserved!

MAVIS. (*Laughs gaily, flinging other arm across his chest, and pillowing her cheek upon his shoulder.*) Why, what a thing to say, Mister Draper!

BARRY. (*As* SUSAN *opens door.*) Oh, please call me "Barry."

MAVIS. *(As* JAMES *steps into room.)* Only if you'll call me "Mavis"! *(Glances up, sees newcomer, straightens self and skirt at once.)* Why, Inspector Crandall! Don't tell me you're hard at work on Sunday?!

JAMES. Crime knows no calendar, Mrs. Hollister. *(To* SUSAN.) But—whom have we here?

SUSAN. I'm Susan Hollister, just back from America by steamship, during which voyage I met and became engaged to Barry Draper, the young man you see there on the sofa.

BARRY. *(Rises.)* Inspector.

JAMES. Mister Draper. Miss Hollister.

SUSAN. *(Shutting door.)* But whatever can a police inspector want of *us?*

JAMES. Then you don't know about your father—?

SUSAN. Oh, that, yes, but I thought Constable Howard was handling the case.

JAMES. Hardly. Constable Howard merely came here to return a missing cat.

BARRY. Are you absolutely sure? I mean, Constable Howard is just now off to the lab with a target pistol found in a secret drawer. Hardly seems an occurrence in connection with a cat.

JAMES. Target pistol?

SUSAN. In the sideboard.

JAMES. Secret drawer?

MAVIS. Same place. But I'm forgetting my manners. Will you stay to lunch with us, Inspector?

JAMES. Sorry, but I never eat when I am on duty.

MAVIS. *(Moves toward sideboard.)* Then how about a drink?

JAMES. Oh, all right.

MAVIS. *(Preparing drink.)* Whisky and soda—?

JAMES. That would be kind of you. *(To Others, as* MAVIS *fixes drink—no ice, these people are British— and brings it to him.)* Now, let me see, where was I?

SUSAN. On duty.

JAMES. Ah, yes! (*To* MAVIS, *as she hands him drink:*) Mrs. Hollister—thank you—I saw Sir Charles yesterday afternoon, with regard to your husband's telephone call to him the night before. (*Takes sip of drink.*)

SUSAN. Sir Charles Rumley? Father's solicitor? (*To* BARRY.) We say "solicitor" when we mean "lawyer."

BARRY. Why?

SUSAN. Why *not?*

JAMES. In answer to your question, Miss Hollister—yes.

SUSAN. Which question?

JAMES. When I said "Sir Charles," did I mean "Sir Charles Rumley."

MAVIS. Don't *you* know?

JAMES. I wasn't asking if that's who *I* meant, I was answering her question about which question *she* meant.

SUSAN. And did I?

BARRY. Did you what?

SUSAN. Mean that question?

MAVIS. I'm sure *I* don't know.

JAMES. Well, I *assumed* she did.

SUSAN. Then I probably did.

BARRY. Did what?

JAMES. Mean it.

MAVIS. Oh.

BARRY. I'm glad that's settled.

JAMES. (*Finishes drink, hands glass to* MAVIS.) Now, where was I?

SUSAN. At Sir Charles Rumley's.

JAMES. Ah, yes!

MAVIS. (*Returning glass to sideboard.*) And what did Sir Charles say?

JAMES. Sir Charles said that— I think you'd all better sit down.

SUSAN. What an odd thing for Sir Charles to say.

BARRY. Susan, I think the inspector said that.

JAMES. I did say that.

MAVIS. That's right, I heard him.

BARRY. In any event, let us sit down. (*Trio sits as before,* JAMES *standing right of sofa, during:*)

JAMES. Now what's all this about a target pistol—?

MAVIS. It was in the sideboard.

BARRY. In a secret drawer.

SUSAN. And it had been fired.

JAMES. Fired?

LOTTIE. (*Off.*) Three times!

JAMES. (*After brief glance toward kitchen, lowers voice.*) I say, can we be overheard in here?

MAVIS. If you like.

BARRY. I don't think he meant that.

SUSAN. Oh, an inspector wouldn't lie.

JAMES. Thank you. Now, let me tell you the terms of Edgar Hollister's will.

BARRY. Just one moment, Inspector. What has Edgar Hollister's will got to do with all of this—the target pistol, the three shots, the missing cat?

JAMES. It is my understanding that Edgar Hollister intended to have it altered!

SUSAN. Mavis's cat!?

BARRY. Of course not, darling!

SUSAN. Well, he can't mean the target pistol!

MAVIS. I believe Inspector Crandall was referring to your father's will.

JAMES. Exactly. And your father told Sir Charles that he wished to draw up a new will with drastically altered terms!

BARRY. Even so, Inspector, I can't see of what importance the terms could be.

JAMES. They could provide a motive.

BARRY. A motive for what? For all we know, Edgar Hollister is alive and well.

JAMES. That's true enough, of course. . . .

MAVIS. Still, as long as you've gone to all that trouble, Inspector, you may as well tell us the terms.

SUSAN. Oh, yes, please do!

JAMES. Well, skipping over minor bequests—charities, social organizations, and servants—

LOTTIE. (*Off.*) Minor, indeed!

JAMES. (*Continues imperturbably.*) Edgar leaves his bride—Mavis Templeton Hollister—this house, the car, and an annual income of one thousand pounds. The remainder of his estate—a not-inconsiderable fortune in the tens of thousands of pounds—goes to his only child, Susan Hollister.

SUSAN. Oh, how darling of Daddy!

MAVIS. (*Concealing her own displeasure.*) Yes. Darling. But—um—Inspector . . . ?

JAMES. Yes, Mrs. Hollister—?

MAVIS. (*Trying to be ultra-casual about it.*) If Susan should—oh—*die* or anything—um—*then* where would the money go?

JAMES. In that event, of course, the money would all revert to you.

MAVIS. (*Barely hiding her delight.*) I see. Of course, it was just a hypothetical question.

SUSAN. Oh, I know that, dear Mavis! And please don't worry about me. I'm very young, and terribly healthy, so I'm certain I shan't die for years and years.

MAVIS. (*Reaches out and fondly pats* SUSAN's *knee.*) I'm sure of it, my darling. And just to be sure, I shall watch over you like a mother hen, every moment you're living here under my roof!

BARRY. *Your* roof—?

MAVIS. Just a figure of speech. But, after all, if anything *has* happened to Edgar—heaven forbid, of course—this *will* be my roof she's under.

BARRY. I guess that's true enough.

SUSAN. (*Dimpling with delight.*) I say, Mavis—do you mean to tell me that, even though this house should become your own, you would let me continue to live on?

MAVIS. (*Jolted by the phrasing.*) Live on?

SUSAN. Live on *here*, as your houseguest, I mean.

MAVIS. (*Recovering.*) Oh! Well, yes, of course! Susan, this is your home, where you were born and raised. And here you shall *live* as long as I *like*—that is, as long as *you* like. (*Gives a merry laugh, in which Others join; PHONE rings.*) Here, I'll get that— (*Starts for phone.*) There's no point in interrupting Lottie when she's preparing luncheon! (*Lifts phone, speaks brightly.*) Hallo—?! . . . Oh, yes, he is. Just a moment. (*Hands phone to* JAMES.) It's that young constable. He wishes to speak to you.

JAMES. Thank you. Probably has the report on that pistol. (*On phone.*) Crandall here! . . . *What?* . . . But—are you *quite* certain? . . . Yes. Yes, I see . . . All right, Constable. Thank you. (*Hangs up, turns to look at* MAVIS.) The strangest thing . . . !

MAVIS. What is it, Inspector? Did something odd turn up in ballistics, or *wherever* he was taking that pistol—?

JAMES. Not precisely. He—he never *took* the pistol to ballistics.

SUSAN. (*Rises.*) But I'm certain that's where he'd intended to take it . . . ?

JAMES. And he had. But—you see—he suddenly discovered that there was nothing ballistics could test for him.

MAVIS. What? I—I don't understand.

JAMES. Well—it's the damnedest thing—I mean, after all, it *was* a *target* pistol—so I don't really understand it myself—

MAVIS. Understand what, Inspector—?

JAMES. The pistol was loaded with blank cartridges!

MAVIS. (*A hand going to her throat as the implication sinks in.*) But . . . that's . . . impossible—!

JAMES. Nonetheless, it's true. I guess we can rule out foul play by that pistol. Anyone who might have tried shooting Edgar with *that* would have a rather healthy victim on their hands when they were through.

MAVIS. (*Can barely speak coherently; sways giddily.*) But—I don't understand—that pistol—loaded with blanks—I—I—Ooooooh! (*Her eyes roll up into her head and she faints into* JAMES' *arms.*)

SUSAN. (*Turns to* BARRY, *speaks brightly.*) I must say—*I'm* rather overcome with relief, *myself!*

CURTAIN

ACT TWO

SCENE 1

*About four in the afternoon, the same day. SUSAN has
changed into something casual and cheerful, and
MAVIS is in another absolutely smashing cocktail
gown. Both are seated at the table, on which a
silver tea service now rests, and MAVIS is just
pouring tea into SUSAN's cup as the scene begins.*

MAVIS. There you are, my dear. Do you take cream?
Sugar? Lemon?

SUSAN. No, thank you. It's just fine, as is.

MAVIS. (*Setting down teapot.*) You can't be sure
until you've tasted it, darling. I'm not certain my skill
at tea-brewing is all it should be.

SUSAN. It certainly *was* kind of you to make the
tea, on Lottie's afternoon off.

MAVIS. Well, I thought that—what with the two of
us here, quite alone, it would help pass the time. Now,
drink up.

SUSAN. (*Lifts cup to lips, but sets it down without
drinking; MAVIS, of course, follows every such move-
ment with extreme intensity.*) It's so hard to simply
just *sit* here! Wondering . . . worrying . . .

MAVIS. About what?

SUSAN. Why—Father, of course!

MAVIS. Oh, yes, of course, I'd nearly forgotten.

SUSAN. Forgotten Father?

MAVIS. What I mean, my dear, is that I am so swept
up in my *own* personal concern for him and his where-
abouts that I quite forgot how much *you* must *also* be
concerned. Now, drink up.

47

SUSAN. (*Almost does, but sets cup down again.*) Do you know—I was just wondering—if Father might not be in the cellar!

MAVIS. (*Looks absolutely stricken, but recovers instantly.*) What—what a silly notion! The cellar, indeed! If he were, we'd have found him there!

SUSAN. Oh, but you see—there's a secret room down there. I've only just now remembered it.

MAVIS. You must be mistaken, my dear. Now, hurry, drink your tea before it gets cold!

SUSAN. But Mavis—didn't Father tell you about it? His various secret rooms and drawers and things are his particular pride and joy. I would have thought he'd have shared the secret with the woman he married.

MAVIS. Well—perhaps he *did* say something or other about it— I've been so upset since his disappearance that I can't be expected to recall *everything*.

SUSAN. No, no, of course not, dear Mavis. I quite understand. But I do think it might be worth our while to have just a little peep into the Murder Room.

MAVIS. (*Horribly startled.*) *Where* did you say—?!

SUSAN. (*Gives a tinkling self-deprecatory laugh.*) Oh, that was just Father's little joke. You *know* how funny he is!

MAVIS. Yes. A barrel of laughs.

SUSAN. He always used to josh about the secret room in the cellar, said it would be a perfect spot to hide a body after a murder, because no one knew it was there. So we came to refer to it as the Murder Room. Are you *sure* he said nothing to you about it?

MAVIS. Well. Now. Of course. He *may* have said *something* of the sort . . . ! (*As if she hadn't known it all along:*) Oh, *that* room! Just behind the *wine* rack, you mean!

SUSAN. Yes, that's the one! I thought he might be *hiding* there, perhaps. He does so enjoy pulling one's leg.

MAVIS. I daresay. But in any case, he simply can't be in that room. Constable Howard mentioned quite definitely that the wine rack was solid. It seems to me that the secret door had been nailed shut—yes, that's right, it all comes back to me, now. The panel in the wine rack that used to open into the secret room is nailed firmly shut.

SUSAN. How strange. Do you think we should mention it to the police?

MAVIS. (*A cry of panic.*) No! (*Then a quick recovery.*) I mean, since it *is* nailed shut, he can't have gone behind it, and why should we waste the policemen's time following false leads?!

SUSAN. That's true, I suppose.

MAVIS. Besides, if he *had* been accidentally nailed in there, I'm certain he would have pounded upon the back of the wine rack to be let out—after all, he'd surely suffocate if he'd been nailed in there— (*Brightening as the import of her own words strikes home.*) even if he were perfectly healthy when he was first sealed in! Yes, of course! Even a healthy man would suffocate there in a day's time!

SUSAN. Oh, but Father wouldn't let that happen to him.

MAVIS. My dear, I don't see what he could do about preventing it.

SUSAN. Well, obviously, if he *had* been accidentally locked in there, he'd simply come popping out of the *other* secret door! (*Goes to sip her tea, but* MAVIS *grabs her hand.*)

MAVIS. *Other* secret door? What are you saying? *What* other secret door?

SUSAN. Why—at the foot of the secret stairway, of course. Didn't Father tell you?

MAVIS. (*Now in a barely concealed state of panic.*) No. No, he never mentioned it. Not a word. I had no idea there was—another way out of that room. . . .

SUSAN. Oh, I'm *so* glad I could cheer you up this way!

MAVIS. (*In a daze.*) What—? Cheer me up—?

SUSAN. Why, yes. I can see your mood is much more alive than when we first sat down to tea, so I can only assume it has done wonders for your spirits to know that, if Father *had* been locked in there, he's certainly out by now! (*Outside window, we see* ABEL *approaching front door.*)

MAVIS. Yes. Yes, of course. But—Susan—this other exit—where is it—?

SUSAN. Let me think. It seems to me that the secret exit was—um— (*DOORBELL rings.*) Oh, there's the door! Shall I get it? (MAVIS *rises.*)

MAVIS. No-no, I will. I can't imagine who'd be calling on us at this time— (*She is moving doorward as she speaks, and just as her hand takes hold of the knob:*)

SUSAN. Perhaps it's Father!

MAVIS. (*Almost crumples, knees buckling, but manages to straighten.*) I do wish you hadn't said that! (*DOORBELL rings again;* MAVIS *leans very near to door, whispers:*) Who is it—?!

ABEL. (*Off.*) Constable Howard of the Harrogate Police, Ma'am!

MAVIS. (*The Law is better than the Walking Dead, after all.*) Oh, how nice, it's only the police! (*Opens door.*) Good afternoon, Constable!

ABEL. (*Entering.*) Good afternoon, Ma'am. . . . Miss.

SUSAN. Good afternoon, Constable. To what do we owe this unexpected pleasure?

ABEL. (*Moves toward table while* MAVIS *closes door.*) There've been a few new developments in the case, Miss Hollister. I wanted to discuss them with you.

MAVIS. (*Following him to table.*) And not with me?

ABEL. Oh, sorry, I was using the word in its plural sense. With *both* of you, naturally.

SUSAN. (*Gesturing him to vacant chair.*) Won't you join us? We were just having tea.

ABEL. Why, thank you, Miss. Very kind of you, I'm sure. (*Sits where indicated as* MAVIS *sits in her own chair again.*) I do hate to miss my tea, but with all this work I thought I'd have to pass it by.

SUSAN. (*Extends her own cup and saucer.*) Here, take this, I haven't touched it—

MAVIS. (*Lurches for it.*) *No!*

SUSAN. What—?

ABEL. I say—!

MAVIS. (*Setting cup on tray, putting her own there, and picking up entire silver service on tray.*) It's cold! That's what it is! Cold! Can't give you cold tea! I'll just go make some fresh!

SUSAN. But really, Mavis, darling—

ABEL. There's no need—

MAVIS. Nonsense! Least I can do! I won't be a minute! (*Flees with tray to kitchen.*)

ABEL. Is—is your stepmother always this jittery, Miss?

SUSAN. Oh, I'm *sure* not. It's just worry about Father. It would make anyone a bit jumpy. Do you know, I thought she'd faint when I suggested that it might be Father at the door just now.

ABEL. Is that a fact! She—she must be very anxious, mustn't she . . . !

SUSAN. Oh, I expect it's just all the talk about the secret room.

ABEL. Secret room, did you say?!

SUSAN. Oh, dear, I promised her I wouldn't mention it to the police! (*He looks at her in surprise.*) Now-now, it's nothing like that! We simply didn't want you to waste time on a false trail.

ABEL. Oh, I see. And what makes you so certain it *is* a false trail, Miss?

SUSAN. Well, because even if Father *had* accidentally gotten nailed into the room behind the wine rack, he'd simply have popped out the secret stairway.

ABEL. Room? Behind the wine rack? Secret stairway?

SUSAN. Oh, *please* don't say anything to Mavis! I *did* promise her I wouldn't bother you with all this!

ABEL. No, Miss. Of course not, Miss. But—some other time—would you mind just showing *me* where this secret stairway is—?

SUSAN. If you like. But I don't see—?

ABEL. Ssh! Here she comes! Not a word, now, we don't want to upset her.

SUSAN. You're *so* understanding! (*Looks up brightly as* MAVIS *re-enters emptyhanded.*) Hallo, Mavis! Back so soon?

MAVIS. The—the water is heating up for the tea. What have you two been chatting about—?

SUSAN. The weather!

ABEL. Yes, the weather!

MAVIS. What *about* the weather?

SUSAN. Nice!

ABEL. Ever so nice!

MAVIS. That's nice. (*Sits at table again.*) But you said you had news for us, Constable—?

ABEL. Well, it may mean nothing, of course . . .

SUSAN. Even so, I should like to hear it.

ABEL. Quite so, Miss. It's about your father's disappearance.

MAVIS. Well, naturally! What else *could* it be?

ABEL. I don't mean about *his* disappearance, specifically, Ma'am, I mean the actual *act* of *disappearing*, itself.

MAVIS. Oh?

SUSAN. I'm afraid you have me at a loss, Constable.

ABEL. Well, it's like this: In order for a person to disappear, he must *be* in a place, and then *not* be in that place, do you see? Our problem is, if he went off, *how* did he go off?

MAVIS. Does it really matter so much?

ABEL. Possibly not, but it does give us food for thought, if you follow me.

SUSAN. I'm not sure I do.

ABEL. All right. Let's say he's vanished.

MAVIS. He *has* vanished.

ABEL. Yes, Ma'am, but I wish to present this as a hypothesis.

MAVIS. Oh, very well.

ABEL. Well, then—*how* did he go about vanishing? There's only the one car—and *you* were driving that, right?

MAVIS. Um . . . yes . . . ?

ABEL. And there were no trains out of here that night, and none of the cab companies has any record of a passenger answering to your husband's description, nor is there any record of a car coming by the house here before your own did, that night—

SUSAN. Can you be quite sure of that?

ABEL. That's what Lottie assures me, Miss. Seems she's a light sleeper, and headlights of any car approaching the house awaken her.

MAVIS. Perhaps a car came while it was still light out. It *is* July . . . the sun seldom sets before eight o'clock or so . . .

ABEL. Yes, but in that case, Lottie wouldn't have been to bed at *all*, yet, do you see?

MAVIS. He—he might have *walked*—

SUSAN. Without anyone seeing him? Oh, no, Mavis, I think not. Father is a rather well known personage hereabouts. Someone would have remembered.

ABEL. As a matter of fact, someone *did* remember seeing him, Miss.

SUSAN. There, now! What did I tell you!

ABEL. But he wasn't walking.

MAVIS. What—*was* he doing—?

ABEL. Cycling. On a lady's bicycle. After dark.

SUSAN. Father? On a lady's bicycle? Whatever for?

ABEL. I'm afraid we're not certain about that, Miss. From reports of three independent witnesses, he seems to have been following a cat.

Susan. But that's absurd. Why would Father follow a cat about?

Mavis. You—don't suppose it was *my* cat he was following, do you—?

Abel. Ah, that's very astute of you, Ma'am! As a matter of fact, that's just what we *did* think. Especially after finding your cat dead of cyanide poisoning, you know.

Susan. Mavis's cat? Poisoned?

Mavis. I'm afraid, dear, in the excitement of your father's disappearance, I forgot to tell you about that.

Abel. That's quite understandable.

Mavis. Thank you.

Susan. But in any case, we've cleared up the means of Father's disappearance. With no car, or train, or cab, he went off by bicycle!

Abel. The only trouble with that theory, Miss, is that the bicycle was found *here*, out back in the garage.

Mavis. Nonsense! You can't *know* it was the same bicycle.

Abel. The three witnesses' descriptions tally . . .

Susan. In every respect—?

Abel. In every one. (*Ticks them off on his fingers.*) Golden handlebars . . . bright red handgrips . . . turquoise frame . . . orange fenders . . . mink fur seatcover . . . revolving tail-lights . . . three-tone bell . . . polka-dot chain guard . . . and lemon-colored pedals

Mavis. There must be *hundreds* like it!

Abel. Well, of course, there *could* be, Ma'am . . .

Mavis. I'm *sure* there are.

Susan. Yes, I saw one just like that this very afternoon.

Mavis. There, you see?

Abel. Where was that, Miss?

Susan. In our garage.

Abel. Miss—perhaps you don't understand—

MAVIS. (*Rises.*) I'll just go see about that tea, Constable—

ABEL. What? Oh, yes, the tea. Thank you, Ma'am. Now—um—what was I just talking about?

SUSAN. I can't recall.

MAVIS. Well, it probably wasn't important. Excuse me, while I get the tea. (ABEL *half-rises respectfully as she exits, then he sits again.*)

SUSAN. I wonder where Father *went* on that lady's bicycle . . . ?

ABEL. Oh, we know that right enough, Miss. He left it outside a two-flat building on Sudbury Lane. (*There is a CRASH in the kitchen;* ABEL *and* SUSAN *rise.*)

SUSAN. Mavis—?

ABEL. Everything all right, Ma'am—?

MAVIS. (*Off.*) Y-yes. Just fine. I dropped the tea service, is all.

SUSAN. Oh, what a pity!

ABEL. Oh, don't worry, Miss, I can get a cup when I return to town.

MAVIS. (*Enters from kitchen.*) It's a terrible mess, I'm afraid. I hope Lottie doesn't have too much trouble cleaning it up. (*Sits at table,* SUSAN *does, too, but* ABEL *remains standing.*) But won't you please continue, Constable—?

ABEL. I'm afraid that's all I have to report for now, Ma'am. I'll keep you advised of any further developments, of course. (*Starts for door,* MAVIS *and* SUSAN *rising as they see him go.*)

SUSAN. I'm dreadfully sorry about your tea, Constable. I hope we may do better the next time you join us—?

MAVIS. Susan, it isn't likely the constable will be joining us for tea again.

SUSAN. Oh, but surely he wouldn't hold dropping the silver service against you?

MAVIS. Darling, I mean that in the normal course of

events, the constabulary does not pop in socially to hobnob with people in exclusive neighborhoods.

ABEL. (*At front door, opening it as they come up to him.*) Your stepmother's right, Miss. It *is* a bit unusual, if you take my meaning.

SUSAN. I'm sorry, I didn't know. That's what comes of receiving my higher education in America.

ABEL. Oh, that reminds me, Miss—what's become of your friend, Mister Draper?

SUSAN. Barry? Oh, he was seeing about taking a room at the hotel in town. I expect him to drop by any time, now.

ABEL. But *you* are staying on *here?* Just you, alone with your stepmother?

MAVIS. Is there anything wrong in that?

SUSAN. And I'm not *alone*, not really, not with Lottie here. Of course, she's not here today.

ABEL. (*Standing hesitantly in open doorway.*) I see.

MAVIS. (*Puts a hand to the door, preparing to shut it.*) Well, I'm certain you must be very busy, Constable, so we'll let you be on your way—

ABEL. Oh, I just remembered! There *was* one *more* bit of information I *forgot* to give you.

MAVIS. And what was that—?

ABEL. It probably means nothing, but—

SUSAN. Oh, do tell us, regardless.

MAVIS. Yes, do.

ABEL. Well, it seems one of the witnesses was the woman who lives in the first-floor flat of that building on Sudbury Lane. She saw Mister Hollister leaving, and—

SUSAN. And—?

ABEL. He did an odd thing.

MAVIS. He did?

SUSAN. An odd thing?

MAVIS. How odd!

SUSAN. What thing?

ABEL. He removed the name of the tenant of the second-floor flat from its position near the bell-push.

MAVIS. He—did *what?*

ABEL. Removed the name and put it into his pocket.

SUSAN. What an odd thing to do.

ABEL. We thought so, yes.

MAVIS. Constable—I was wondering—did your witness happen to notice—um—what sort of jacket he was wearing at the time?

ABEL. Matter of fact, yes, she did, because it was so unusual.

SUSAN. What was unusual about it?

ABEL. It was a rather expensive smoking jacket. Hardly the sort of thing one wears on the trail of a fugitive cat after dark.

SUSAN. It certainly doesn't sound like the sort of thing Father would do.

MAVIS. No, it's not at all like him to do such a thing. Which makes me suspect that either the witness is in error, or that man was not Edgar!

ABEL. Oh, it was Mister Hollister, right enough. The witness is certain of that. She even stepped out into the foyer and watched him get upon his bicycle, and she could see his face quite clearly beneath the street lamp.

MAVIS. And—this second-floor flat on Sudbury Lane—what have you done about that?

ABEL. Why—nothing. What *should* we do about it?

SUSAN. Didn't you even ascertain who lived there?

ABEL. Do you think we *should* . . . *?*

MAVIS. *No!* . . . I mean, I'm sure it wouldn't be of any help to you. After all, if Edgar was seen leaving the place, he obviously hadn't disappeared as yet, so I'm sure whoever lives there could be of no help in your investigation!

SUSAN. I never thought of that. You're quite right, of course.

MAVIS. Of course I am.

ABEL. Now that I think of it, I don't suppose it would do any harm to look into the identity of the tenant in that flat, just in case—

MAVIS. Just in case what?

ABEL. Why, he might have mentioned where he was going next, don't you see?

MAVIS. But you've already as good as said he came straight back here! You did say the bicycle was in our garage, didn't you?

ABEL. By Jove, you're right! Well, then, I suppose it would be a waste of time disturbing whoever lives there, wouldn't it!

MAVIS. Yes, it would. A terrible waste of time. You really mustn't bother! (*Starts pushing* SUSAN *and* ABEL *through door, babbling.*) Susan, why don't you walk Constable Howard to his police car, or bicycle, or whatever he came with, like a good little hostess?!

SUSAN. Oh, certainly, Mavis, whatever you like. Come, Constable! (*Links her arm in his, leads him out.*)

ABEL. (*Back at* MAVIS, *who is rapidly closing door.*) Good afternoon to you, Ma'am!

MAVIS. Good afternoon! (*Slams door, watches out window as* SUSAN *and* ABEL *appear there for a moment, waves gaily, they wave back, and then the instant they are out of sight she gallops to phone, yanks it up, and dials furiously; then, on phone:*) Hallo! Darling! . . . It's *Mavis*, of course, whom did you *think?!* . . . That dreadful constable is going to investigate the second-floor flat on Sudbury Lane! . . . Yes, *your* flat! . . . How soon can you move out? . . . But he mustn't see *you* there—if he should *connect* the two of us—! . . . Well, then, what *are* you going to do? . . . (*Listens intently; nods; nods again; shakes her head in vehement negative; shrugs; then nods again.*) All right, darling, if you think it will work . . . Oh, by the way, Susan said something about a secret exit from that room in the cellar where we put you-know-who the other night . . . No, she didn't . . . Well, of *course* I shall question her further! What do you think I *am?!* . . . (*Smiles, obviously flattered by the*

BARRY. Oh, very well, I'll stroll on back to town and tell the Reverend Smithers to hold off.

SUSAN. It's only for a day or so, my darling. And I do so want Daddy there.

BARRY. I understand, Sweetheart. Well—I'm off to town! (*Starts out door, but pauses as PHONE rings.*) Perhaps that's for me—I told Sir Charles to phone if there were any problems he hadn't thought of.

SUSAN. Oh, and perhaps Reverend Smithers can't have the church ready on time, today, so it might also be *him.* (*PHONE rings again.*)

BARRY. On the other hand, it won't matter if he can't, since we're not going to be married this afternoon, after all.

SUSAN. Yes, that's true . . . (*PHONE rings again.*) Still and all, I do wonder who it could be!

MAVIS. Suppose I answer it and see. (*Picks up phone.*) Hallo—! . . . What? . . . Who is this?! . . . Who—?! . . . Oh, no! No! (*Drops phone receiver to floor, stands swaying, dazed.*)

BARRY. (*Solicitously.*) Wrong number—?

MAVIS. (*Wide-eyed, still swaying.*) No . . .

SUSAN. Then . . . who *is* it?

MAVIS. It's . . . it's *Edgar!* (*Swoons and sprawls untidily onto floor.*)

SUSAN. I say, what marvelous luck! Perhaps we **can** be married today, after all! Shall I speak to Father and ask him?

BARRY. By all means, darling!

SUSAN. (*Lifts phone, speaks into it.*) Daddy? Daddy, darling? . . . Daddy, are you there? . . . (*Slumps prettily.*) Oh, blast, he's rung off! (*As she hangs up phone, LOTTIE—in coat and hat—enters from kitchen, one hand pointing back toward it.*)

LOTTIE. Who did that to my kitchen?! (*Sights MAVIS, swings hand to point toward her.*) And who did that to my floor?!

SUSAN. Mavis fainted and fell when Father phoned.

BARRY. (*Playfully.*) I'll bet you can't say that three times, fast!

SUSAN. (*Blank.*) What?

BARRY. (*Dashed.*) Oh, nothing.

LOTTIE. Well, here, we can't have her cluttering up my clean floor. Will you give me a hand, young man? (BARRY *applauds enthusiastically.*) Now, really—!

BARRY. (*Dashed again.*) Sorry. Just my American whimsicality popping out at the wrong moment. (*He and* LOTTIE *get still-unconscious* MAVIS *to her feet.*) Thanks, Lottie. I think I can manage alone from this point—!

SUSAN. (*As he swings* MAVIS *up into his arms.*) Be careful, darling! . . . Don't wrinkle her dress!

BARRY. (*Staggering slightly under load.*) I'll try not to. Lottie, where shall I put her?

LOTTIE. (*Ponders slowly.*) Well, I suppose hearing from her missing husband must have given her quite a shock, so she'll be needing a good rest to recover from it, but I don't think the sofa is comfortable enough for that sort of thing, and the armchair is a bit small, and—

BARRY. (*Trying not to gasp, gasps:*) Lottie . . . anywhere . . . !

SUSAN. (*Helpfully.*) Her bedroom's just at the head of the stairs—

BARRY. (*Reeling but still game, lurches toward landing.*) *Those* stairs—?!

SUSAN. They are a bit steep, aren't they?!

LOTTIE. Oh, here, let me help! (*Takes* MAVIS's *ankles, and* BARRY *holds* MAVIS *under the arms, backing upstairs and out of sight, with* LOTTIE *following, at the same time we see* ABEL *approaching front door.*)

SUSAN. (*Calls up stairs after the struggling duo, sweetly.*) There are smelling salts in the medicine cabinet!

BARRY. (*Off. Grunting with his burden.*) Thanks! I

can use some! (*Before* SUSAN *can clarify her meaning,
DOORBELL rings.*)

LOTTIE. (*Off. Also grunting.*) Miss Susan, would you
get the door—?

SUSAN. What do you need the *door* for?

BARRY. (*Off.*) She means *answer* it!

SUSAN. Oh, of course, how silly of me! (*Flits prettily
to door, flings it wide.*) Why, Constable! I thought you
were interrogating the tenant of that second-floor flat
on Sudbury Lane!

ABEL. (*Will enter, and she will close door, during:*)
As matters turned out, I couldn't, Miss. Tried to, of
course, but something unexpected went up.

SUSAN. You mean "came up."

ABEL. No. "Went up." A quarantine sign on the
door. Measles. Didn't want to take a chance. I've
never had the measles.

SUSAN. Oh, what a pity.

ABEL. How do you mean that, Miss?

SUSAN. Oh, quite sincerely. But—what brings you
back here, Constable?

ABEL. Well, as long as I had nothing better to do, I
thought I might pop back and ask you about that
secret stairway.

SUSAN. Oh, by all means, do! (*Just stands there,
smiling prettily.*)

ABEL. (*When he sees she is unlikely to volunteer
information.*) Yes. Well. Just where *is* this secret
stairway, Miss?

SUSAN. (*Points to windowseat.*) Right under there!

ABEL. (*Takes an uncertain step that way.*) You
mean the windowseat, Miss?

SUSAN. Yes. It opens up, and there's a stairway just
underneath it, and at the bottom of the stairway
there's a secret door into the Murder Room.

ABEL. (*Reacts.*) *What* did you say—?!

SUSAN. (*Recites from memory.*) Yes. It opens up,

and there's a stairway just underneath it, and at the bottom of—

ABEL. (*Interrupts quickly.*) I don't mean *everything* you said. I mean what you called it.

SUSAN. Called what?

ABEL. The Murder Room.

SUSAN. *That's* what I called it.

ABEL. Uh. Yes. So you did. But what I wondered was—*why?*

SUSAN. Why what?

ABEL. Did you call it that.

SUSAN. The Murder Room?

ABEL. Yes.

SUSAN. Because that's what *Daddy* always called it. He thought it would be a perfectly smashing place to hide a body from detection, if one *had* a body one did not *wish* detected, of course.

ABEL. Ah! Yes, it's perfectly comprehensible when you once explain it.

SUSAN. What *isn't?!*

ABEL. Yes. Well. Let's just have a *look* at this stairway of yours—! (*Starts for windowseat, then abruptly stops.*) I say—no one's likely to be popping up while I look, is there?

SUSAN. You mean out of the windowseat?

ABEL. Well. That, of course, but—I actually meant into this room. I wouldn't want anyone to see me nosing about.

SUSAN. Whyever not?

ABEL. Well, I don't have a warrant, or anything, and—till there is absolute *proof* of foul play—I might have a difficult time getting one, but till I get one, I shouldn't be nosing about, and yet I really *ought* to nose about in order to *get* proof of foul play, but you see—until there *is*—I can't get the warrant I need to *prove* that there is.

SUSAN. How's that again?

ABEL. (*Gives up.*) Never mind (*Bends, tries to lift*

ABEL. (*Similarly.*) He's not calling *me*, he's questioning *you!*

SUSAN. (*Similarly.*) About what?

ABEL. (*Similarly.*) What *you* said to *him!*

BARRY. (*Off.*) Susan, why don't you answer me—?!

SUSAN. (*Calls prettily.*) Would you mind repeating the question?

BARRY. (*Off.*) What question?

SUSAN. (*A whisper again.*) What question?

ABEL. (*Sincerely.*) I forget.

BARRY. (*Off, but his voice is nearer.*) Susan, who in the world are you talking to?

SUSAN. What makes you think I'm talking, darling?

BARRY. (*Off.*) I can hear your voice, for one thing. (*We hear his footsteps on the stairs.*) Susan, would you mind telling me—

ABEL. (*A hoarse whisper.*) Stop him!

SUSAN. Barry, darling, don't come down, please!

BARRY. (*Off. Footsteps cease.*) Why not?

SUSAN. (*Brightly.*) Because I'm dressing! (ABEL *covers his eyes with one hand in despair; she misinterprets, whispers:*) Not *really*, Constable.

BARRY. (*Off.*) In the living room?!

SUSAN. (*To* ABEL, *in a whisper.*) What shall I answer?

ABEL. (*Just about giving up, uncovers eyes, shrugs, whispers.*) Don't ask *me!*

SUSAN. (*Naturally takes this as a suggestion, calls up to* BARRY:) Don't ask *me!*

BARRY. (*Off. We hear footsteps on stairs again.*) Susan, what on earth are you talking about—?!

ABEL. I've got to hide!

SUSAN. Where?!

ABEL. The secret stairway!

SUSAN. But it's closed!

ABEL. Well, open it! (*Rushes toward windowseat;* SUSAN *does rigmarole; lip pops up;* ABEL *clambers inside and crouches down.*)

SUSAN. (*Urgent whisper.*) *Now* what?
ABEL. *Close* it, you imbecile!

(SUSAN, *highly insulted, gasps in outrage and starts toward him; this, of course, permits lid to shut, and from inside windowseat, we hear* ABEL *scream, and his scream mingles with THUMP-CRASH sequence as on cellar steps, and just at end of this,* BARRY *descends stairs into room, having seen nothing.*)

SUSAN. (*Brightly.*) Hallo, darling!
BARRY. (*Looks about, puzzled and blank.*) Weren't you just talking to somebody?
SUSAN. Yes, darling.
BARRY. Who?
SUSAN. You, darling. Don't you remember?
BARRY. I mean somebody down here!
SUSAN. Darling, you *are* down here!
BARRY. Yes, but I wasn't a moment ago!
SUSAN. (*Slides into his arms.*) And I missed you so! (*Cuddles against him, cheek against his chest.*) I say, darling, have you had the measles?
BARRY. (*Absently patting her back as they cuddle, still looking about in curiosity and bewilderment.*) Not recently.
SUSAN. But at some time or other?
BARRY. I seem to recall that I did. Of course, I was a child at the time.
SUSAN. (*Straightens briskly, steps back from embrace.*) Good! Then let's go to a certain second-floor flat on Sudbury Lane!
BARRY. Whatever for?
SUSAN. (*Pauses, ponders, then smiles prettily.*) To ask the man with the measles for facts about Father! (*Takes step toward door, then stops instantly and turns, for:*) And I *won't* say that three times, fast! (*And as she links her arm in his and tows him doorward—*)

BLACKOUT

ACT TWO

SCENE 2

Early that same evening, just after dark. Drapes are drawn. Room is illuminated with both FULL LIGHTS and LAMPLIGHT. MAVIS, in an elegant negligee and slippers, is on phone, her expression anxious.

MAVIS. . . . Operator, are you *sure* it doesn't answer—? . . . Yes, yes, I did try dialing it myself, but when I couldn't get a reply, I thought that perhaps *you* could . . . But there *must* be somebody there! . . . All right. All right. Thank you, anyway. (*Hangs up, stands there, distraught, fingertips at temples.*) He must be there. He can't have gone out. He would have told me.

LOTTIE. (*Steps in from kitchen, in work dress and apron.*) Did you call, Mrs. Hollister?

MAVIS. Yes, but there's no answer!

LOTTIE. I mean, did you call *me*, just *now?*

MAVIS. What? . . . Oh! . . . No, Lottie, no, I didn't . . . Are—are you *sure* there haven't been any phone messages for me since this afternoon—?

LOTTIE. No, Mrs. Hollister.

MAVIS. No *what?* No, you're not *sure?*

LOTTIE. No, there have been no messages.

MAVIS. Not—not even from Susan and her young man—?

LOTTIE. Nothing, Missus.

MAVIS. (*Pacing back and forth, a nervous wreck.*) I don't understand it! I just don't understand it! (*Stops and confronts* LOTTIE.) They said *nothing* about where they were going?

LOTTIE. I'm sorry, they didn't. Master Barry helped me carry you upstairs, and Miss Susan waited here, and when I came down, they'd both gone. (*Before* MAVIS *can speak again, we hear a distant nerve-*

grating SCREECH—the sound made by a long nail being prised out of thick wood—and both women look toward cellar door.)

MAVIS. There it is again! Did you *hear* it, Lottie! Did you *hear* it?

LOTTIE. Yes, Mrs. Hollister, I heard it. That makes nine.

MAVIS. (*Raging.*) Did I *ask* you to count!? Must you keep on totaling up the number of those terrible screeching sounds we've heard this evening?!

LOTTIE. I'm sorry, Missus. It was only—no, never mind.

MAVIS. Only what?! Tell me what?! What do you know that I don't?!

LOTTIE. Well, Missus, it's just that—on the day Mister Hollister disappeared, I had just bought ten new tenpenny nails, and when he vanished, why, the nails had vanished with him.

MAVIS. (*Gets startled and guilty look, then hides it.*) Nonsense! Don't be ridiculous. You simply miscounted.

LOTTIE. Oh, no, Mrs. Hollister. I'd never miscount tenpenny nails, they're too expensive.

MAVIS. Lottie, a tenpenny nail is called that because of its *length*, not its *price!*

LOTTIE. (*Straight out front, in quiet realization.*) I've been swindled. (*Exits to kitchen.*)

MAVIS. (*Babbling to herself.*) Some day that woman will drive me mad! Perhaps she already has! I must be imagining things—no, wait—she heard the sound, too! But—it can't be what I think it is! It must be the house settling! That's it! It's an old house. They always make noises at night. That's what it is. Yes. (*Freezes in position, mouth agape, as we hear SCREECH again; then a distant hollow BOOM, as of a thick door opening; MAVIS breaks from her paralysis, rushes to cellar door and flattens her palms against it, trembling.*) No! No, I won't listen! It's nothing! Nothing at all! (*Far below, we hear a hollow*

FOOTFALL on the cellar stairs; MAVIS *takes a backward step toward kitchen; another FOOTFALL; she takes another backward step, then turns and shrieks.)* LOTTIEEEEE—!

LOTTIE. *(Off.)* Did you call, Mrs. Hollister?

MAVIS. Lottie, get out here! Come here at once, do you hear! I need you! *(Another FOOTFALL, and she turns, flattening herself against Upstage end of sideboard, staring in horror at cellar door.)* Lottie—!

LOTTIE. *(Off.)* Now-now, Missus, there's nothing to be afraid of, I'm sure. *(Another FOOTFALL.)*

MAVIS. *(Eyes riveted to cellar door.)* Then why aren't you here?!

LOTTIE. *(Off.)* Because, Missus, I'm under my bed. *(From this point, FOOTFALLS—about two seconds apart—come up cellar stairs, nearer and nearer, without pause, during:)*

MAVIS. *(Frightened out of her wits.)* No! No, please! Stop! Go back! Back where you came from! Stay away! *(PHONE rings, she screams at the sudden sound, FOOTFALLS cease; PHONE rings again;* MAVIS, *revitalized, dashes to phone, grabs it up, her back toward cellar door.)* Darling! Darling, is it you, at last?! . . . What? . . . Who? . . . *(Then in total nonfright and utter exasperation.)* Reverend Smithers?! What in blazes do *you* want?! . . . Bridesmaids? What bridesmaids? . . . Waiting for *whom?!* . . . Oh, damn and blast, didn't they tell you the bloody wedding has been postponed?! . . . Till *hell* freezes over, for all I care! . . . *(Behind her, cellar door slowly opens, and a hand—and we can recognize the cuff and sleeve of the smoking jacket from Act One— gropes for the lightswitch on the wall behind her.)* Yes, off! . . . Yes, that's what I said! . . . Now, will you please ring off! I am expecting a very important call, and—! *(Stops in shock as hand flicks switch, and FULL LIGHTS go out, leaving only pool of LAMPLIGHT at left end of sofa.)* What—? What's happened to the lights—? (*Suddenly senses a presence, turns in apprehensive terror.*) Who's that? . . . Who's there? . . . (*Sees and recognizes cuff and sleeve.*) No! No, it can't be! Go away! Don't come near me! (*Door slowly swings open, as she cringes backward, unable to leave the spot, a bubbling moan rising from her throat, and then she and we see the person—eyes fixed upon her, and teeth bared in a fiendish grin—at the same moment, and she shrieks:*) EDGAR—! (*At this instant, front door opens, and* SUSAN *and* BARRY, *with* JAMES *right behind them, step into room, along with a howl of night WIND, which starts the lamp toppling, during:*)

SUSAN.   Hallo, everybody, we're   home—! . . . DADDY!

(*Toppling lamp hits sofa and LAMPLIGHT goes out, leaving room in total DARKNESS; we hear* MAVIS *SCREAM, we hear cellar door SLAM, and then FULL LIGHTS come up suddenly, via* BARRY, *who has pushed lightswitch above stair landing; cellar door is shut;* MAVIS *is unconscious on floor beside dangling-and-oscillating telephone receiver;* SUSAN *is still staring toward where she saw her father, jaw agape; even normally imperturbable* JAMES *is supporting himself against frame of open front door, his face a study in stricken horror;* LOTTIE *enters from kitchen.*)

LOTTIE.   Miss Susan! What's happened? (*As she rushes forward,* SUSAN *topples into dead faint into* LOTTIE'S *arms with a little moan,* JAMES *manages to come back erect again and move shakily into room, shutting door without turning to look at it, and* BARRY *rushes to help* LOTTIE *with* SUSAN, *who hangs like a dead weight between them as they drag-carry her toward sofa, where they will lay her down, next to toppled lamp, head Left.*)

JAMES. Brandy! Lottie, where do you keep the brandy?!

LOTTIE. The sideboard! Oh, Susan, my sweet child, wake up, darling, wake up!

BARRY. Now-now, she's all right, just had a nasty shock, Lettie.

LOTTIE. Lottie.

BARRY. Lottie.

JAMES. (*Opens Upstage cabinet door on sideboard, takes out tray with brandy decanter and six small stemware goblets.*) Here we are! This should fix us all just fine! (*Will set tray atop sideboard, starts filling goblets.*)

BARRY. (*Chafing* SUSAN'S *wrists.*) Susan—it's Barry —wake up, sweetheart! Please wake up!

MAVIS. (*Moans, trembles, then blinks instantly awake, sits up.*) Edgar—! What—? Where—?

JAMES. Don't try to talk, Mrs. Hollister, you've had a bad fright.

MAVIS. (*Getting groggily to her feet.*) But—I thought—I thought I saw—no, I'm certain I saw—!

JAMES. Yes-yes, I know. We *all* saw him! (*Drains goblet of brandy, shivers.*)

LOTTIE. What? Saw who? I didn't see anybody.

BARRY. Then take our word for it! It was Edgar Hollister!

MAVIS. In the flesh!

JAMES. We hope! (*Drains second goblet.*)

SUSAN. (*Moans, tosses head from side to side, then sits up.*) Daddy—?! . . . Oh, I .must have been dreaming—?!

BARRY. Don't worry, darling, everything's all right!

JAMES. Then stop chafing her wrists! (*Drains third goblet.*)

BARRY. (*Stops.*) Oh. Sorry.

SUSAN. (*Inspecting wrists.*) My, but that smarts! Whatever did you *do* to me?

LOTTIE. He was chafing your wrists, Miss Susan.

SUSAN. Why?

BARRY. It's—it's the thing *to* do with a person who's fainted. I'm not entirely certain why.

LOTTIE. The pain wakes them up.

MAVIS. (*As* JAMES *raises fourth goblet and drains it.*) Inspector, may I *please* have one of those before you finish off everything!

JAMES. Oh. Sorry. Here you are! (*Hands her fifth goblet, then turns and drains sixth.*) Ah! I needed that!

MAVIS. Don't you mean "those"?!

JAMES. Whatever. I must apologize, but—really—it gave me an awful turn.

BARRY. (*Straightens up as* SUSAN *swings her feet to the floor.*) Inspector Crandall . . .

JAMES. (*Setting down final empty goblet as* MAVIS *drinks her brandy.*) Yes, Mister Draper—?

BARRY. Why?

JAMES. (*Stares;* MAVIS *pauses in mid-swallow, suddenly tense.*) I—I don't follow that. Why what?

BARRY. Why did it give you an awful turn to see Edgar Hollister?

JAMES. Because—because—*oh* . . . Oh, yes, I see what you mean.

SUSAN. *I* don't. Barry, what *do* you mean?

BARRY. Well, if I were to walk into a man's home, and see the man of the house standing before me, I don't think *I* would go into sudden shock. As a matter of fact, that's just what I *did*, and I *didn't!*

LOTTIE. How's that, again?

BARRY. (*Impatiently.*) Did come in, and didn't go into shock!

JAMES. I must apologize. I can tell you why I reacted that way. If you must know, I had already convinced myself that Edgar Hollister was dead, murdered by person or persons unknown. So, naturally, when I saw him—

MAVIS. Of course! That makes splendid sense.

BARRY. Well—I suppose it *might* have that effect on a person . . .

MAVIS. Might? What of your own fiancee? Didn't she faint, too?

SUSAN. Mavis is right, darling. It *was* a shock, and I had only a *suspicion* that Daddy had met with foul play.

LOTTIE. But what about Mrs. Hollister? Moaning and pacing and screaming the house down, and then flopping unconscious like a heap of wet wash!

MAVIS. Nonsense! I was waiting by the telephone for some word from Susan, and I must have fallen asleep on the floor.

BARRY. The telephone! Is there somebody still on the line—? (*Dashes to phone, puts it to his ear.*) Hello—? . . . Reverend Smithers! How are you? . . . Oh, I'm sorry to hear that. . . . *What* woman—? . . . She said *that* to you? Yes, it *must* have been a shock!

LOTTIE. Said what?

SUSAN. What woman?

BARRY. (*Waves them silent.*) Sssh! . . . No, not you, Reverend . . . What? . . . Well, yes, she was quite right about that. We decided to hold the wedding off until Susan's father was available for it—

SUSAN. (*Jumps up from sofa.*) But he *is*, darling, he *is!* We *saw* him here, just moments ago—!

JAMES. Miss Hollister—I hardly know how to tell you this, but—do you know—it may *not* have been your father whom you saw.

BARRY. (*On Phone.*) Yes, we'll surely let you know soon what we decide. It would be a shame to keep you waiting by the phone all night! . . . Thank you. Give my love to the bridesmaids! (*Hangs up.*)

SUSAN. *Not* my father, Inspector? But—I certainly know my own father when I see him!

MAVIS. The room was dark. You could have been mistaken.

LOTTIE. But—why would anyone *pretend* to be Mister Hollister—?

JAMES. That's just what we don't know. And, therefore, until we do, I am afraid I shall have to take Susan into protective custody.

BARRY. But we don't know that the imposter is *dangerous* . . . ?!

MAVIS. We don't know that he *isn't!*

SUSAN. We don't even know that he's an *imposter!*

LOTTIE. And if it *is* her father, what has she to fear?

MAVIS. Ah, but that's just the point. Edgar, remember, was about to make an alteration in his will! Even if it *is* Edgar—do any of us *really* know how safe that is for Susan?

SUSAN. (*Indignantly.*) Daddy would never harm a hair of my pretty little head!

LOTTIE. Of course not!

JAMES. Nonetheless, it's better to be safe than sad—!

SUSAN. (*Corrects him.*) "Sorry."

BARRY. For what?

SUSAN. "Sad."

LOTTIE. *What's* sad?

SUSAN. The word he said instead of "sorry."

JAMES. Oh. Sorry.

MAVIS. That's better.

SUSAN. Than what?

BARRY. "Sad."

LOTTIE. Well, certainly. Anyone would rather be sorry than sad.

JAMES. "Safe than sad."

SUSAN. "Safe than sorry."

MAVIS. Oh, shut up, all of you! I have a beastly headache, and I'm going to bed! (*Starts for stairs.*)

JAMES. And I shall take Susan into custody.

SUSAN. Oh—very well, if you insist. (*Rises from sofa.*) I say, Mavis—? (MAVIS *pauses on stairs.*) If Daddy *does* show up, will you please tell him where I am?

MAVIS. Certainly, darling. But—exactly where *will* you be—?

BARRY. The police station, I suppose—?

JAMES. No-no, too dangerous. That's the *first* place a maniac would *look!*

LOTTIE. Then where? The local hospital?

SUSAN. No-no, that's the *second* place a maniac would look! . . . I wonder what the *third* could be—?!

BARRY. How about the church basement?

LOTTIE. The back room at the beauty parlor!

SUSAN. The projection booth at the cinema!

LOTTIE. (*Points at* BARRY.) The butcher shop!

BARRY. (*Points at* LOTTIE.) The dentist's office!

SUSAN. (*Pat-a-cakes hands.*) The candy store!

MAVIS. (*Has been watching this rapid-fire pingpong of suggestions in growing exasperation, and finally cannot stand it.*) STOP! (*Others all look her way in respectful silence, so she speaks her next line gently.*) Suppose we let the *inspector* tell us what he has in mind—?

JAMES. Thank you. (*To Others.*) I propose to take Susan to the one place she can be perfectly safe!

OTHERS. And where is *that—?!*

JAMES. My apartment.

LOTTIE. *What?!*

MAVIS. I *say!*

SUSAN. How *dare* you!

BARRY. *See here*, now—!

JAMES. (*Raises a hand, they all fall silent.*) Properly chaperoned, of course.

MAVIS. Oh, good!

LOTTIE. *That's* a relief!

SUSAN. *I* should *say* so!

JAMES. Then why not *do* so?

SUSAN. "*That's* a relief!"

LOTTIE. That's what *I* say!

JAMES. That's what you *said!*

SUSAN. And so did *I!*

LOTTIE. That makes *two* of us!

MAVIS. *What* does?

JAMES. *That.*

MAVIS. Oh.

BARRY. But—chaperoned by *whom—?*

JAMES. Why, by Mrs. Hollister, of course.

MAVIS. Oh, I should adore that! Where could Susan be safer than with *me!* (*Will exit up stairs on:*) Let me just change into something suitable for chaperoning!

JAMES. And I'll just bring the car around here to the front door! (*Exits out front door.*)

LOTTIE. I wonder—should I fix you something to eat, first, Miss Susan—? It may be a long and tiresome journey.

BARRY. Oh, there's no need, I'm happy to say. It's not far at all.

LOTTIE. Oh, then you *know* where the inspector lives?

BARRY. Yes, we've all just come from there, in one of our bungling amateur attempts to solve this case.

LOTTIE. And where is it?

SUSAN. (*Her eyes dancing prettily.*) It's a lovely little second-floor flat on Sudbury Lane!

CURTAIN

ACT THREE

*It is shortly before midnight, the same day. LAMP-
LIGHT—the lamp has been replaced on the
table—bathes sofa area, but the rest of the room
is much dimmer. BARRY is seated on sofa, a large
tablet of paper on the coffeetable before him, a
large pencil in his hand. He stares at paper,
bemused, pondering. LOTTIE enters from kitchen
in nightgown and slippers.*

LOTTIE. Will there be anything else, Master Barry?
Another sandwich? More milk?
BARRY. Hmm? Oh! No, thank you, Lettie.
LOTTIE. Lottie.
BARRY. Lottie. No, you can toddle off to bed.
LOTTIE. But sir—I can't go to bed until I've locked
up for the night.
BARRY. Oh, of course. Well, then, why don't you do
so?
LOTTIE. Because *you're* still here, sir.
BARRY. What? Oh, my gracious, do you know—I
completely forgot that I don't live here! (*Gives self-
deprecatory laugh.*) That's what you get for making
me feel at home. (*Rises, stretches, yawns.*) I suppose
I might as *well* go back into town and get some shut-
eye. I'm certainly getting nowhere with my amateur
detecting! (*Tosses pencil onto tablet.*) It's just—
there was something about Inspector Crandall's *face*
tonight—I can't put my finger on it—!
LOTTIE. No one likes a finger in the face.
BARRY. No-no, I mean, something I *didn't see*
there—!
LOTTIE. *What* didn't you see?

79

BARRY. That's the problem—I can't remember, although it struck me quite forcefully at the time . . .

LOTTIE. It's odd, isn't it, sir, that each of us knows there's something strange going on, and yet none of us can quite explain why we think so.

BARRY. Yes. That *is* disturbing. But I'll be damned—

LOTTIE. (*Shocked.*) Oh!

BARRY. —darned—

LOTTIE. (*Puzzled.*) Eh?

BARRY. —dashed—

LOTTIE. (*Contented.*) Ah!

BARRY. —if *I* can make heads or tails of it all! Well, maybe if I sleep on it, some sort of solution will present itself. (*Starts for front door.*) Good night, and thank you again. (*Starts to open door.*)

LOTTIE. Good night, sir. And be careful walking into town this late at night. No telling *what* kind of horrible creatures might be lurking in the fog, with knives, or guns, or—

BARRY. (*Shuts door instantly, but speaks as if casually.*) Do you know, I was just wondering—I don't suppose you have a spare room where I might spend the night—?

LOTTIE. Well, there's Mrs. Hollister's room—or Miss Susan's—but I don't know if I should let you use them without permission . . .

BARRY. How would it be if I slept on the sofa?

LOTTIE. Uncomfortable. That sofa's much too short for you. Of course, if you scrunched up a bit—

BARRY. Then it's settled. That's what I'll do. (*Moves back down into sofa area.*) I don't suppose you could lend me a toothbrush?

LOTTIE. I'm sorry, sir. I never brush my teeth. (*When he looks a question at her:*) I wear dentures.

BARRY. Really? I'd never have guessed. Remarkable work they do nowadays. (*Sits on sofa.*)

LOTTIE. Yes, no one is quite what they seem, anymore, thanks to artificial enhancements. Why, you'd be amazed how exactly natural-looking were that wig and mustache of Mister Hollister's—

BARRY. (*Stares at her, then slowly stands.*) What's that you say—? Wig and mustache—? What do you mean?

LOTTIE. I mean that when he wore them, their falseness was undetectable. You'd have sworn they were his very own hair.

BARRY. But damn it all—darn it all—*dash* it all—why would Mister Hollister wear a false mustache and wig?

LOTTIE. Solely for Miss Templeton's benefit, I believe.

BARRY. You mean Mavis?

LOTTIE. Yes, sir. He was afraid she might be a fortune-hunter.

BARRY. So he wore the false hairpieces to discourage her?

LOTTIE. Oh, no, sir, quite the reverse.

BARRY. I'm afraid I don't follow that, Lettie.

LOTTIE. Lottie.

BARRY. Sorry.

LOTTIE. That's all right.

BARRY. Thank you.

LOTTIE. Don't mention it.

BARRY. Where were we?

LOTTIE. You were afraid you didn't follow what I said about Mister Hollister wearing the mustache and wig to *encourage* Miss Templeton, rather than the reverse.

BARRY. Yes, why should such a getup impress her favorably?

LOTTIE. Because they made him seem an *older* man, sir. To Mister Hollister's way of thinking, a fortune-hunting woman would be drawn to a man who didn't seem to have too many years left.

BARRY. Yes—yes, I can see how that might appeal to her. But—really, now—if he thought she *was* a fortune-hunter, why would he do the very thing that would be likely to *win* her? Why not act his own age and severely disappoint her ambitions?

LOTTIE. It was her legs, sir.

BARRY. Her legs?

LOTTIE. Shapely, he called them. He was quite taken by them. Even if the woman were a fortune-hunter, he hadn't the heart to let go those legs.

BARRY. Let them go?

LOTTIE. He always *did* enjoy pulling people's legs—in more ways than one.

BARRY. (*Muses aloud, slowly sitting back down on sofa.*) Yes. Yes, I begin to see. And I find it quite interesting! Do you know, Lottie, you may just have solved the entire mystery!

LOTTIE. Go on with you, sir! What are you talking about—?! (*Sits beside him on sofa, fascinated.*) How could what *I* just have said have solved the *mystery?!*

BARRY. Don't you *see*, Lottie—?

LOTTIE. (*Automatically, from too much practice correcting him.*) Lettie.

BARRY. "*Lettie*"?!

LOTTIE. I mean, "Lottie." You confused me when you got it right the first time. But tell me how I solved the mystery!

BARRY. Well, we've been looking at the thing *backwards!*

LOTTIE. How so, sir—?

BARRY. We've been operating under the assumption that Mavis was madly in *love* with Edgar Hollister. But if what you say is true, then she wasn't in love with Edgar at all, only attracted by his money!

LOTTIE. (*Catching his drift.*) So—if she had married him thinking him an old man—and learned that he was actually a young man, a man who would live on for years and years—

BARRY. Exactly! She would *do* something about it! I can see it now—there the two of them are, on their wedding night—she believes she is with an elderly gentleman who is likely to pop off his mortal coil momentarily, and then suddenly he whips off the wig, and—

LOTTIE. No, wait, sir, it couldn't have happened that way.

BARRY. Why not?

LOTTIE. Because they weren't *together* on their wedding night!

BARRY. What—? But whyever not?

LOTTIE. She said she was going to a meeting over at Reverend Smithers' church.

BARRY. A fortune-hunter? Going to church? Wouldn't that strike Edgar as odd?

LOTTIE. Do you know, sir, that's undoubtedly what *did* happen? Which explains the potassium cyanide in the cocoa! Oh, I should never have washed out the pan!

BARRY. Cyanide? What are you talking about? Pan? Cocoa? I don't follow you!

LOTTIE. She wasn't going to church at all! She merely wished to be away from the house when the poison did its work, so she mightn't be suspected of having administered it!

BARRY. No-no, that can't be! Something's wrong here! If she put the poison into the cocoa *before* she went out, then she must *already* have known that Edgar wasn't the old crock he pretended to be, but if she'd married him only that morning, when had she time to discover the truth?

LOTTIE. She hadn't. Not on her own, at any rate!

BARRY. Then—you think—

LOTTIE. Somebody must have told her! Somebody who knew Mister Hollister's actual age!

BARRY. But that could have been anybody! He was a well known personage in this area. Susan said so. He must have been acquainted with people by the *dozens* who knew the truth.

LOTTIE. Yes, but *Miss Templeton* wasn't! She is not

originally *from* this area. So she would know *no one* well enough to tell her his actual age!

BARRY. (*Stands, abruptly.*) Wait! It's all coming together! A fortune-hunter—marrying what she imagined was an old crock—she wouldn't love *him* at *all*—but, *therefore*—being rather a hot number, *herself*—*!*

LOTTIE. (*Stands just as abruptly.*) She must have had a boy friend on the side!

BARRY. And he must have known Edgar's actual age!

LOTTIE. And that's how she found out, and put the poison in the cocoa! (*Both give whoops of elation, clasp hands, and dance in a happy circle; then, when back in original spots:*)

BARRY. But wait—who *is* Mavis's boy friend? The man she *really* loves?!

LOTTIE. There's a simple enough way to find out! (*Starts Upstage toward phone.*)

BARRY. (*Following her, at sea.*) There is?

LOTTIE. There is if you understand women! (*Lifts phone, dials once for the operator.*) There are only two motivations to a woman's character: Being in love and talking about it! And the one way in which a woman can indulge both interests simultaneously is—

BARRY. (*Snaps fingers as he gets it.*) Making phone calls to her lover! Of course! Why didn't *I* think of that?

LOTTIE. Because you don't understand women!

BARRY. What man *does?!*

LOTTIE. (*On phone.*) Hallo, Operator? . . . This is Mrs. Molloy, housekeeper at Bynewood Cottage. I wonder if you could clarify an item on our telephone bill? . . . Well, there's a number I don't recognize, one that has been called quite frequently since this last Friday morning . . . Yes, that's the number! Can you tell me whose it is? . . . Oh, what a pity!

BARRY. What's the matter?

LOTTIE. (*Covers mouthpiece.*) It's unlisted! (*Back*

on phone.) Well, could you at least tell me the address from which that number originates—? . . . *What?* . . . Are you *quite* sure?! . . . Oh, my stars! (*Hangs up, turns frantically to* BARRY.) Master Barry—!

BARRY. (*Clutches her hands.*) What *is* it?!

LOTTIE. I forgot to tell the operator *"thank you"!*

BARRY. (*Drops her hands.*) Oh, *blast* the operator! What's the bloody *address?!*

LOTTIE. It's a lovely little second-floor flat on Sudbury Lane!

BARRY. Inspector Crandall's!? But—*Susan* is there!

LOTTIE. And so is *Mavis!*

BARRY. (*Outraged.*) But—that's two against one!

LOTTIE. Not if *we* get there in time! (*Starts for kitchen.*) Come on, there's not a moment to lose!

BARRY. (*Following.*) Where are we going?

LOTTIE. My bicycle's out back! You can pedal and steer, and I'll ride the handlebars! (*They go dashing off, and we hear back door SLAM; an instant later, front door pops open and* SUSAN *rushes in.*)

SUSAN. Barry? Lottie? I'm home! Are you there? (*Shuts door, steps further into room, puzzled by silence.*) Yoo-hoo . . . anybody home—? (*There are a few heavy THUMPS from windowseat; she opens drapes.*) Oh, my goodness! It's Constable Howard! Hold on, I'll get you out! (*Goes through rigmarole, lid opens and* EDGAR HOLLISTER, *as we first saw him, emerges from windowseat;* SUSAN, *babbling onward as she comes down to him, does not notice at first.*) There you are! All free again! That's why I came back, you know. I was just sitting down with Mavis to have a cup of cocoa at Inspector Crandall's second-floor flat on Sudbury Lane when I remembered I'd never let you out of the secret room, so I jumped up and took the runabout, and drove back here, and— Oh! It's *not* Constable Howard! (*Cringes in pretty fearfulness.*) *Who* are *you—?!*

EDGAR. I am your father.

SUSAN. (*Uncringes prettily.*) Oh, how rippingly splendid! And here I thought you'd been done in! (*Flits momentarily into his embrace, planting a quick kiss upon his cheek, then unembraces him and blinks prettily.*) But—whatever *has* become of Constable Howard?

EDGAR. There is no time to explain now. Mavis and the inspector are right behind you! (*She gives a pretty yelp and twirls about.*) No-no, not in location, in *time!* Surely they will be following you in the inspector's car. They daren't let you get away!

SUSAN. What? But—whyever not? I do not understand, Daddy dearest!

EDGAR. (*Moves swiftly across room to sideboard, which he will bump with his hip as* SUSAN *did earlier to open secret drawer, during:*) There is too much to tell, and too little time to do it in. You must trust me, my darling, and do precisely what I tell you—! Ah! (*Goes to now-open drawer, removes pistol, shuts drawer.*) This time this pistol is not loaded with blanks!

SUSAN. (*As he starts back toward windowseat.*) That pistol! Where did it come from? I thought Constable Howard had it down at the police station!

EDGAR. (*Stands atop closed windowseat, facing into room.*) All in good time, my child! Now, I must hide, and I am trusting you not to betray my presence when Mavis and her lover arrive! (*Draws drapes shut in front of self.*)

SUSAN. Her lover? Daddy! You don't mean—Inspector James Crandall?!

EDGAR. (*Pokes head out between closed drapes.*) I do! Now do you understand your danger?

SUSAN. I can't say as I *do . . . ?!* In any case, I don't think it's sporting of you to leave me here to face them alone and unarmed.

EDGAR. You are not alone, and I am not unarmed. Now be still, I hear them coming! (*Ducks back out of sight behind drapes, and a fearful* SUSAN *drops down prone on floor between sofa and coffeetable, and then* MAVIS *and* JAMES *enter through front door and close it.*)

MAVIS. Susan—? Susan, darling, are you here—? . . . Lottie—? . . . Anybody—?

JAMES. (*Smilingly removing a pistol from inner jacket pocket.*) I guess there's nobody home except for you and me— (*Trains pistol on drapes.*) and Edgar Hollister! (*Drapes rustle.*) Don't move! I have a gun on you! Come out with your hands up! (*Drapes open, and* EDGAR—*pistol in hand, but with hands up—steps down off windowseat into room, scowling at* JAMES.)

EDGAR. Before you shoot me—may I ask—how did you know where I was hiding?

MAVIS. Edgar, you dumdum—those drapes hide you from people in this *room*, not from anyone approaching from the *outside!* We saw you before we even came *in!*

EDGAR. Drat! Never thought of that!

JAMES. Now, will you kindly drop that pistol? I have the feeling it is now loaded with something more deadly than blank cartridges!

EDGAR. Oh, very well! (*Tosses pistol with deliberation onto sofa;* SUSAN, *raising up a trifle, sees it and takes it, unnoticed by* MAVIS *or* JAMES, *then scrunches down out of sight once more.*) Well, let's not waste any time. Take me far away from this house and finish the job you only thought you did two days ago!

MAVIS. (*Laughs.*) Oh, Edgar, your ruses are so transparent! Naturally, it will do us no good to take you away until we have Susan in our power as well! I don't know how we arrived here before she did, but this is certainly the spot to which she shall come!

JAMES. Exactly! And when we have finished off the two of you, all the money shall come to Mavis, and then she and I can be wed and live our lives as extremely wealthy people with barrels of money!

EDGAR. (*Laughs scornfully.*) Money?! You fools, there *is* no money!

JAMES. Sir Charles Rumley wouldn't lie to a police officer! He assured me your estate was several thousands of pounds!

EDGAR. Oh, it is!

MAVIS. Well, then—?

EDGAR. What you two seem to have overlooked is that although the word "pound" may mean a denomination of *money*, it is also a denomination of *weight!*

MAVIS. What?

JAMES. Weight?

EDGAR. Yes, you fools! Bynewood Cottage stands on my estate. I had an agricultural engineer estimate the tonnage of its topsoil week before last. It came to several thousands of pounds!

JAMES. Curses! We've been tricked!

MAVIS. But—why? Edgar, how could you have known in time to trick us?

EDGAR. Inspector Crandall confided in me that he had an amorous attachment to a certain man's bride-to-be only last Tuesday. The very next day, chancing to glance through the window of a little tea shop, I saw her with him, and discerned at once that she was my very own Mavis.

JAMES. Bosh and balderdash! I would never have confided such a thing to you!

EDGAR. Ah, but you did not know it was I to whom you were confiding it! Because at that time, I was impersonating the man known to you as— (*Whips off wig and mustache.*)

MAVIS. (*Completing his phrase in ghastly shock.*) Constable Howard!

SUSAN. (*Sits up into view, in similar shock.*) It *is* Constable Howard! You lied to me! You said you were my daddy! (MAVIS *reacts.*)

JAMES. (*Holds out his hand, speaking quickly.*) Yes, he *did* lie, you *can't* trust him, but you *can* trust *me*, so just give me that pistol like a good girl! (*She does so at once, dimpling prettily.*) *There's* a love!

EDGAR. (*Stands there till it is much too late, then blurts:*) Susan, don't *do* it!

SUSAN. But I *did* do it!

EDGAR. Blast! *Now* you've done it!

MAVIS. And now you're *done* for!

SUSAN. Oh, what have I *done?!*

EDGAR. You've *undone* us, *that's* what you've done!

JAMES. She's done you *down*, all right! (*Repockets own gun.*)

MAVIS. Oh, let's do them *in*, and have *done* with it! (JAMES *trains target pistol on* EDGAR.)

EDGAR. Wait!

JAMES. Well? I'm waiting—?!

MAVIS. *Why* are you waiting—?!

JAMES. To hear what he has to say.

MAVIS. Well, I suppose even Edgar is entitled to a few last words.

EDGAR. Thank you.

SUSAN. I say, did you say "Edgar"?

JAMES. Of course she did. You little numbskull, he's been your father all along!

SUSAN. (*Rushes to* EDGAR.) Oh, Ninny, I've been such a daddy! (*Frowns prettily, considering her statement.*) Or something.

EDGAR. (*Places fond arm across her shoulders.*) Now-now, don't reproach yourself, Susan, you could not have known the truth.

SUSAN. But—what *is* the truth? How can you be my daddy and Constable Howard, both?

MAVIS. It's really very simple, Susan.

EDGAR. How would *you* know?

MAVIS. The moment I knew you'd loaded that pistol with blanks, I figured the whole thing out!

JAMES. And didn't tell *me?*

MAVIS. There wasn't time.

JAMES. Oh.

EDGAR. But there's plenty of time, now.

SUSAN. So do tell us!

JAMES. Is this a stall for time?

EDGAR. No, it isn't.

SUSAN. Naturally not.

MAVIS. But that's precisely what you'd say if it *were* a stall for time!

JAMES. Still, it's what they'd also say if it weren't.

MAVIS. That's true.

SUSAN. So please *do* explain, and help *me* understand about *everything!*

MAVIS. *That* could take *years!*

EDGAR. She doesn't mean *everything!*

SUSAN. Just about the *mystery!*

MAVIS. Oh, all right.

JAMES. I suppose we may as well. (*Over the explanation—which is spoken quite briskly, without hesitation, by the Others—*SUSAN *will look from one speaker to the other in polite and rapt attention, absorbing all.*) To begin at the beginning, I told Constable Howard I was enamored of Mavis.

EDGAR. Not knowing that Constable Howard and I were the same man.

MAVIS. Because Edgar has always been ashamed of being a police constable.

EDGAR. So I worked on the force under an assumed name.

MAVIS. But on the night when I first shot him—

JAMES. And phoned me to help her hide the corpse—

EDGAR. When I fell and pretended to be killed I struck my head—

JAMES. And knocked himself so unconscious that Mavis and I took him for dead—

MAVIS. When we stashed him in the Murder Room and nailed it shut!

EDGAR. However, when I awakened there I had partial amnesia—

MAVIS. And thought himself to be Constable Howard only—

JAMES. Completely forgetting the Edgar part of his identity—

EDGAR. So that I ended up trying to solve my own murder!

MAVIS. But when was your memory *restored?*

EDGAR. When Susan dropped me down the secret stairway onto my head!

JAMES. Ah, then it was you who phoned the house, here, as your real self!

MAVIS. Completely terrifying *me!*

EDGAR. And I never did take the pistol to ballistics—

JAMES. Because you knew all along that it was filled with blanks!

MAVIS. Because you knew I might try to use it upon you!

EDGAR. Which you did, after failing to feed me the poisoned cocoa!

MAVIS. Some of which I again failed to feed Susan earlier tonight.

JAMES. But when I knew you were investigating my flat—

MAVIS. He put up the "Measles" sign—

JAMES. But Barry had already had measles—

EDGAR. So he dashed over there regardless—

MAVIS. And saw that there was not a single measle on your face—

EDGAR. So he began to suspect you at once—but then he forgot why!

JAMES. And now it's quite too late—

MAVIS. Whatever Barry may suspect—

JAMES. Because we are going to murder the two of you and get it *right* this time!

MAVIS. There, now, Susan, do you understand—?

SUSAN. (*Stands a moment, smiling prettily, then shakes her head.*) Sorry, no. Would you mind telling it again?

JAMES. (*Raises pistol.*) I should mind exceedingly.

SUSAN. Oh, Daddy, must we let them do us in? Must we?

EDGAR. I really cannot see how we can *prevent* them doing so, dearest daughter.

SUSAN. But there must be a way! There simply must!

JAMES. Well, there's not!

EDGAR. But there *could* be—!

MAVIS. Couldn't!

EDGAR. Could!

JAMES. Such as?

SUSAN. Help arriving at the last crucial moment!

MAVIS. You've been seeing far too many American movies!

JAMES. Yes, in real life the cavalry never shows up on time! (*Opens front door, still facing into room, gestures them in door's direction with pistol.*) Now, be quick about it, you two!

SUSAN. (*Huddled against* EDGAR, *not moving.*) I say, where are you taking us?

MAVIS. To the quarry. A few gunshots, some rocks tied to your feet, a lovely splash—and it's all over!

EDGAR. But why? I've already told you there's no money to be gained by this!

JAMES. True or not, we've gone too far to turn back now! Come along!

EDGAR. I guess we'd better go with them, Susan.

SUSAN. Yes, I expect so. But—oh—it would have been *so* lovely if the cavalry *had* shown up—! (*Then All gasp and react in surprise as* BARRY *and* LOTTIE— *he pedaling furiously, she riding on the handlebars— come rolling in through the front door on* LOTTIE'S *bicycle—*)

LOTTIE. Not so fast! Not so fast! (*And they continue rolling right off into the kitchen, from where, a moment later, we hear a loud CRASH.*)

SUSAN. (*Pat-a-caking hands.*) It's Barry! We're saved!

JAMES. (*Still brandishing gun.*) Well, *hardly!* (*As BARRY and LOTTIE trot back into room from kitchen.*) Stop! I have you covered!

MAVIS. James—what shall we do?! We can't fit them *all* into the car!

JAMES. Very well, then, we'll take *both* cars!

SUSAN. No, that won't work. You need one person to drive, one to hold the gun!

JAMES. By Jove, she's right!

MAVIS. What shall we do?

JAMES. Shoot them all *now,* and *then* take them to the quarry! (*Closes door.*)

BARRY. (*Standing alongside LOTTIE, their hands raised, says wryly:*) Thanks a lot, Susan.

SUSAN. You're welcome, darling!

MAVIS. Oh, shut up, all of you! Now, please stand here against the wall, so that James can shoot you. (*JAMES and MAVIS back down to Center Stage Left, near the windowseat; Others line up against Upstage wall—SUSAN in between umbrella stand and coat rack.*)

LOTTIE. I suppose you intend to begin with the youngest—?

SUSAN. Oh, no, they should really begin with the oldest—!

BARRY. In any case, ladies first—!

EDGAR. Shame on all of you! We can at least die with brave smiles on our lips!

SUSAN. Daddy's right!

BARRY. Did you say "Daddy"?

LOTTIE. But that's Constable Howard!

EDGAR. That was just my name on the force.

SUSAN. He's actually my father.

BARRY. (*Delighted, reaches out to shake EDGAR's hand.*) I'm very pleased to make your acquaintance, sir!

EDGAR. (*As they shake.*) And I yours. You seem like a fine upstanding young man!

MAVIS. Well, he won't be standing up much longer! (*As they break handclasp and return to hands-raised stance.*) James, will you get *on* with it!

LOTTIE. Wait! Can't someone at least tell me why we're being murdered by an inspector of police?

BARRY. Yes, it would be the decent thing to do, after all.

MAVIS. But, dash it all, we've just been *through* all that!

SUSAN. Oh, but *please* tell it again! Perhaps this time around, I shall begin to grasp matters.

JAMES. (*Turns slightly Downstage to face MAVIS, meanwhile placing his left foot upon the closed lid of windowseat, leaning left elbow on left knee, and keeping pistol pointed Upstage at group, his face a study in weariness.*) *You* tell them, darling! If I have to hear it once again, I shall go mad!

MAVIS. But, there *is* one small bit of information I should like to have.

EDGAR. And what is that, Mavis?

MAVIS. Susan said there was a secret entrance to the Murder Room. I cannot imagine where such an entrance can be. Where is it?

SUSAN. Oh, it's right inside the—

EDGAR. (*Interrupts swiftly.*) Don't tell her! Show her!

SUSAN. But, Daddy dearest, why should I not simply say where it is?

EDGAR. Because actions speak louder than words!

SUSAN. Oh, yes, of course, I'd forgotten! How silly of me! And here, I nearly simply spoke out and said that the secret entrance was in the—

EDGAR. Susan! Show them! Show them!

JAMES. (*Removing his foot from lid and turning.*) Yes, show us. I'd like to see, myself.

EDGAR. Oh, blast!

SUSAN. Whatever is the matter, Daddy, dear?

EDGAR. Nothing, darling, nothing. It's just that— (*Thinks fast, extemporizes:*) Part of what you must do is indecent for a young girl, and I can't have you do it while Inspector Crandall is looking at you!

JAMES. Oh, certainly not! I do beg your pardon! (*Turns and once more reassumes foot-on-windowseat-lid stance.*)

EDGAR. *Now* show them, Susan!

MAVIS. Yes, will you please get on with it?!

SUSAN. No.

BARRY. What? Susan, do you mean you won't show them?

SUSAN. Not if it's something indecent. I didn't *realize* it—I still don't see *why* it is—but if I am to die, I must at least die like a little lady!

EDGAR. Darling, it's not indecent, I just made that part up.

JAMES. (*Turning to face Upstage again.*) In that case, I'll watch.

EDGAR. No, you mustn't! It really *is* indecent. I just said it wasn't so that Susan would go through with it!

JAMES. Oh, I see. (*Once more reassumes his stance with foot on lid.*)

LOTTIE. All right, Miss Susan, go ahead.

SUSAN. But Daddy said it was indecent!

EDGAR. I lied!

JAMES. Then may I look?

EDGAR. No!

SUSAN. But why not?

EDGAR. Oh, damn and blast!

MAVIS. Wait, *I* have an idea! Why not have Susan do whatever it is, and I will watch, and James won't, and then when she has done whatever it is, I will let her know whether it was indecent or not?!

BARRY. I say, that's very decent of you!

MAVIS. No-no, *I* say that's very decent of *Susan!*

SUSAN. But only if it *is!*

MAVIS. Well, naturally!

SUSAN. Promise?

MAVIS. Yes-yes, I promise! Now will you get on with it?!

SUSAN. Oh—very well. (*Moving in concert with her words.*) First of all, I place my foot here—upon the umbrella stand—and then I take hold of this particular prong of the coat rack—

MAVIS. Yes . . . ?

SUSAN. (*Not moving in concert with her words.*) And then I pull the prong and the door opens.

EDGAR. Well?

BARRY. *Well?*

LOTTIE. *Well?!*

SUSAN. I *think* that's *all* of it.

EDGAR. But aren't you going to *show* her—?!

SUSAN. Oh, how silly of me! Yes, of course! (*Tugs prong, lid flips open,* JAMES *is flung backward toward lamp;* MAVIS *screams, lamp topples, lights go out as lamp hits sofa, and in DARKNESS we hear thundering feet, and:*)

LOTTIE. Get the gun!

BARRY. Get the lights! (*FULL LIGHTS come up;* EDGAR *is at wall switch near cellar;* BARRY *is kneeling astride* LOTTIE *between sofa and dining table, his hands at her throat,* SUSAN *is still in rigmarole position, prong down, and* MAVIS, *standing before sofa, has pistol pointed at* JAMES, *his hands up, also before sofa.*)

JAMES. Don't shoot! It's me!

MAVIS. Sorry, darling!

SUSAN. (*She takes a step forward, releasing prong, on:*) I say—! (*Lid slams shut,* MAVIS *twirls toward it.*)

MAVIS. What was that?!

EDGAR. (*Lurches for switch again, and DARKNESS envelops room; again we hear thundering FOOT-FALLS—probably a few grunts and gasps, too—and amid the confusion, still in darkness, hear:*) Get the gun!

MAVIS. Get the lights! (*FULL LIGHTS come up;* JAMES *is at wall switch near cellar;* LOTTIE *is kneeling astride* EDGAR *between sofa and dining table, her hands at his throat;* BARRY *is in rigmarole position, prong up, and* SUSAN, *standing before sofa, has pistol pointed at* MAVIS, *her hands up, also before sofa.*) Don't shoot! It's me!

SUSAN. Sorry, darling! (*Lowers gun,* BARRY *takes step forward, bending prong down, on:*)

BARRY. I say—! (*Lid pops open,* SUSAN *twirls toward it.*)

SUSAN. What was that?! (JAMES *lurches for switch again, and DARKNESS envelops room; again we hear thundering FOOTFALLS, grunts and gasps, and:*)

MAVIS. Get the gun!

SUSAN. Get the lights! (*FULL LIGHTS come up;* MAVIS *is at wall switch near cellar,* JAMES *is before sofa with pistol in his hand, and All Others are facing him just Left of dining table, their hands up.*)

ALL OTHERS. Don't shoot! It's me!

JAMES. Sorry, darling!

ALL OTHERS. Get the lights!

JAMES. (*As* MAVIS *automatically lurches for switch.*) No, don't—! (*But she does, and DARKNESS envelops room.*)

BARRY. Get the gun!

JAMES. Get the lights! (*FULL LIGHTS come up;* SUSAN *is at other switch on stair landing;* MAVIS *is kneeling astride* JAMES, *hands on his throat;* BARRY *is in an amorous embrace with* LOTTIE, *kissing her madly, near telephone;* EDGAR *is seated in armchair, reading his newspaper; then All But* SUSAN *look up, blinking, and:*)

ALL BUT SUSAN. Who's got the gun?!

SUSAN. (*Brings non-lightswitch hand from behind back and before face, and sees that she holds the pistol.*) Oh, dear! *I* have! (*Reaches for lightswitch.*)

BARRY/LOTTIE/EDGAR. Susan, don't! (*She hesitates.*)

MAVIS/JAMES. Susan, do! (*She proceeds; DARK-NESS again; footfalls, grunts, etc., and:*)

WOMEN. Get the gun!

MEN. Get the lights! (*FULL LIGHTS come up; MAVIS is at cellar switch, and also has the pistol; SUSAN is on floor being strangled by BARRY; LOTTIE is in armchair with newspaper; EDGAR and JAMES are madly embracing just below coffeetable; All But MAVIS hold stances for one beat, then all spring to their feet, and—except for JAMES, of course—raise their hands over their heads, keeping their backs to the audience.*)

MAVIS. The first one who moves gets a bullet between the eyes!

JAMES. (*Starts toward her.*) Darling, thank heavens we're finally back in command!

MAVIS. (*Brings gun up.*) Hold it right there!

JAMES. (*He stops, startled, raises his own hands.*) Mavis, are you mad?!

MAVIS. I'll say I am! Good and mad!

JAMES. I didn't mean that kind of madness!

MAVIS. Well, *I* did!

JAMES. But . . . surely . . . you can't be mad at *me—?!*

MAVIS. Can so!

JAMES. Can't!

MAVIS. Can!

JAMES. But—why?!

MAVIS. Because it was *you* who got me *into* this mess in the *first* place! Plying me with your reptilian charm, talking me out of love for a decent man like Edgar, not letting me know he was actually young and handsome without his wig and false mustache and just my type, making me marry for money when I could have married for love, forcing me into nearly committing a murder, getting me into all sorts of trouble with the law, and *now* quietly expecting me to take your part in this miniature massacre! *Ha!*

EDGAR. But—I say, Mavis—precisely what *do* you intend to do?

MAVIS. I intend to shoot you all, close up the cottage, and move to some other town where I can lead a decent, normal life!

JAMES. Impossible!

MAVIS. And why, may I ask?

EDGAR. After murdering five people, no one can lead a decent, normal life. (*Gun dips.*)

BARRY. Yes, it would be a terrible weight upon the conscience. (*Gun droops.*)

LOTTIE. You'd spend the rest of your days in misery and remorse. (*Gun hangs by* MAVIS'S *side.*)

MAVIS. . . . *Reallly—?* (*All But* SUSAN *start to lower hands.*)

ALL BUT SUSAN. Yes, really!

SUSAN. Oh, but, I say—! Aren't we all forgetting something?

JAMES. *What*, my dear—?

SUSAN. (*Brightly.*) A murderess *has* no conscience!

MAVIS. (*Gun coming back up instantly.*) By Jove, she's right!

ALL BUT SUSAN. Thanks a lot, Susan!

EDGAR. Wait! Before you kill us all, Mavis—there is something I must do!

MAVIS. What?

EDGAR. Let me put the lamp back upon the table.

MAVIS. Why?

EDGAR. It looks so sloppy upon the sofa.

MAVIS. Oh—very well.

JAMES. Don't let him do it!

MAVIS. Why not?

JAMES. It may be a trick!

EDGAR. Inspector, whose side are you *on*, anyhow?!

JAMES. Oh, dash it all, I completely forgot! . . .

Mavis, darling, I was wrong, it's not a trick, let him go ahead.

EDGAR. That's better. (*Starts for lamp.*)

SUSAN. Oh, Daddy, I'm so disappointed in you!

EDGAR. (*Pauses, hand upon lamp.*) Disappointed in me? Whatever for?

SUSAN. For not playing a trick on her!

EDGAR. Susan—did it ever occur to you that perhaps I *am* going to trick her?

SUSAN. Oooh, Daddy, that would be jolly fun!

MAVIS. Now, wait, I don't intend to put up with any trickery! Let that lamp alone!

EDGAR. (*Backs from lamp.*) Oh, all right. Go ahead and shoot. I don't care. It's a shame, though.

MAVIS. (*Brings gun up to shoot him, then pauses, then lowers it.*) What is?

EDGAR. That once you shoot me, you'll never find the secret safe with all the emeralds in it.

BARRY. Secret?

LOTTIE. Safe?

JAMES. Emeralds?

SUSAN. In it?

MAVIS. You're bluffing! There's no such safe!

EDGAR. Of course not. Go ahead and shoot.

MAVIS. (*Brings gun up, then wavers.*) Oh . . . damn you! Where's the secret safe?!

EDGAR. It's very difficult to open. I made it that way on purpose.

LOTTIE. It would be stupid to make a secret safe that was *easy* to open!

MAVIS. Stop this chitchat and open it! I want to see those emeralds!

EDGAR. Oh, very well! Susan, you pick up the lamp, and put it on the table. (*She does so.*) Barry, you sit exactly in the center of the sofa. (*He does so.*) Lottie, you press your fingertips against the edge of the dining table. (*She does so.*) Inspector, you go over in the corner and pick up the potted philodendron. (*He does so.*) And now—if Mavis will permit me—I shall open the safe. . . .

MAVIS. Just a moment—I don't completely trust you—tell me, first—exactly where *is* this secret safe?

EDGAR. (*Gestures toward wall behind her.*) In the most logical place in the room—behind the portrait of my late wife. When I trigger the mechanism, the portrait will slide down and expose the safe to view.

MAVIS. Oh, very well, Edgar! Do so!

EDGAR. Thank you, my dear. Susan, lift the lamp straight above the table, and hold it steady there, exactly two inches above the surface! (*She does so.*)

SUSAN. And now what, Daddy, darling?

EDGAR. When I give the signal, I want you to set the lamp down, Barry to stand up, Lottie to push the table four inches toward the sideboard, and the inspector to drop the philodendron! Does everybody understand? (*All ad-lib comprehension.*) Very well, then—on your mark—get set— *Now!* (SUSAN *drops lamp,* BARRY *pops up from sofa,* LOTTIE *lurches against table,* JAMES *drops philodendron, and portrait of Lydia Hollister moves—except that it does not slide down wall, but swings outward on a pivoted base, coming down like a toppling wall-ironing-board onto* MAVIS's *head; she drops the gun, her eyes crossing, and crumples to the floor, the gun being grabbed up by* EDGAR, *who gets the drop on* JAMES.) There, that's much better!

JAMES. (*Glancing tearfully at blank wall back of portrait.*) There's no safe! No emeralds! No nothing!

SUSAN. Oh, Daddy, isn't it delicious! Your first wife took care of your second! (*Rushes to him.*)

EDGAR. (*Pillows her head upon his shoulder.*) Yes. I like to think—Lydia would have wanted it this way . . . !

LOTTIE. Can I stop pushing this table, now?

EDGAR. What? Oh, certainly, certainly! (*As she straightens,* BARRY *comes over and takes* SUSAN's *hand.*)

BARRY. (*Shyly.*) You know, darling—we never *did* tell Reverend Smithers to call off our wedding—!

SUSAN. Oh, darling, do you mean—after all that's happened—you still want to go through with it?

BARRY. Yes, darling, I do.

SUSAN. (*Flits into his embrace.*) Oh, good! That means *you're* as crazy as *I* am!

LOTTIE. Oh, Miss, may *I* stand up for you?

SUSAN. I'd *love* to have you in my wedding party, Lottie. Then, afterward, you can sweep up the rice from the church steps!

LOTTIE. (*Sniffles happily.*) You always *were* a good girl!

JAMES. I say—might *I* stand up for you, too—? I mean, Barry doesn't know anybody in town, and he'll need a best man—!

BARRY. That's awfully decent of you, Crandall— oh, but, will my future father-in-law allow it—?

EDGAR. (*Drops gun from its entrainment upon* JAMES.) Of course I will. Obviously the man's a reformed character, now that Mavis has turned on him and shown her true colors, so he won't have any more motivation for trying to kill me off, anymore, so I daresay I shall be safe enough in permitting him to go off with you, and take part in— (*Stops, because Others have all walked out the front door while he was babbling on, without giving him a backward glance.*) Oh, dash it all, they've departed!

MAVIS. (*Raises up from floor, bright and alert.*) Darling! We're alone at last! (*Comes rushing into his arms, and embraces him.*) Our plan worked perfectly!

EDGAR. Plan? What plan? What are you talking about, Mavis?

MAVIS. Why, darling, our plan to get my lover to

give me the gate, so that you and I could live happily ever after, don't you remember?

EDGAR. Hold on—are you telling me that you're *not* a murderess, a woman whom I should turn in to the police station and have locked up for trial and—later on, of course—public execution?

MAVIS. Yes! That's what I'm telling you!

EDGAR. But the gun—you fired it at me—?!

MAVIS. Knowing all along that it was loaded with blanks!

EDGAR. But the cyanide in the cocoa—?!

MAVIS. It wasn't real cyanide.

EDGAR. But the cat died—?!

MAVIS. Darling, that was a *stuffed* cat, not a *real* one! You just didn't happen to be here when Constable Howard brought it back!

EDGAR. But, dash it all, *I'm* Constable Howard.

MAVIS. Of course you are, but you didn't *know* it, then!

EDGAR. By George, you're right! I forgot about my amnesia!

MAVIS. Amnesia makes it easy to forget.

EDGAR. And—you say—this was all planned between us, you and I—?

MAVIS. Of course, darling, but that nasty old amnesia made you forget the whole thing, and you thought your darling adoring wife was a mean old murderess!

EDGAR. (*Tosses pistol onto sofa, takes her in his arms.*) Dash it all, darling, can you ever forgive me—?! Silly of me to be so forgetful!

MAVIS. Of course I can! Now, how about a nice hot cup of *cocoa?!*

EDGAR. (*Cheek to cheek with her, eyes out front, so that he cannot see her fiendishly calculating smile.*) Hmmm! Don't mind if I do! Perhaps with a dash of brandy? That is, if you *don't* mind putting a little something extra *in* it—?

MAVIS. Believe me, darling, *nothing* would please me more! (*Goes flitting gaily out to kitchen.*) I'll just be half a moment—!

EDGAR. (*Seating himself at Upstage place at dining table.*) Marvelous woman, Mavis! One in a million! So lucky to have found her! (MAVIS *flits right back in with cup of cocoa on saucer, sets it down before him on table, stands smilingly behind him.*)

MAVIS. There you are, dearest! Sorry to take so long!

EDGAR. Ah, but I'm sure it's well worth the wait! (*Drains contents of cup, sets it down in saucer, sighs happily.*) You certainly can cook a corking good cupful of cocoa!

MAVIS. I'll bet you can't say that three times!

EDGAR. (*Wags a finger at her like a mildly autocratic schoolmaster.*) No-no, dearest, you mean, you'll bet I can't say it three times, *fast—!*

MAVIS. (*Smiles warmly.*) No-no, dearest, I mean, I'll bet you can't say it three times, *period!*

EDGAR. (*Blankly, out front.*) Of *course* I can! (*Rattling it off by rote.*) You certainly can cook a corking good cup of cocoa, you certainly can cook a corking good cup of cocoa, you—certainly—can—can cook—can cook a— (*Glances with a frown into cup, then out front, still frowning, then his eyes widen more in surpirse than terror.*) Oh . . . *dash* it all! (*And as he stares and she smiles radiantly—*)

CURTAIN

PROPERTY LIST

ACT ONE

SCENE 1:

Preset
whisky bottle on sideboard
pistol hooked onto Upstage side of sofa

EDGAR
drink in hand at start of scene

MAVIS
handbag and latchkey

SCENE 2:

Clear
pistol from sofa

Preset
pistol in secret drawer for Scene 3

JAMES
business card in pocket

ABEL
large stuffed cat with horrorstruck look

SCENE 3:

Preset
whisky
soda siphon
glasses on tray on sideboard

LOTTIE
wristwatch on wrist

SUSAN
two small suitcases

BARRY
two large suitcases

ACT TWO

SCENE 1:

Clear
  suitcases
  tray
  whisky
  siphon
  glasses

Preset
  silver tea service
  cups on tray on table

SCENE 2:

Preset
  tray with brandy decanter and six *very small* stemmed
  liqueur glasses (or James will never be able to drain five
  of them) in cabinet of sideboard

ACT THREE

Preset
  lamp restored on endtable
  tablet of paper and pencil for Barry on coffeetable
  pistol once more back in secret drawer

JAMES
  second pistol in inner jacket pocket

MAVIS
  cup of cocoa from kitchen

Mechanical Devices
  movable coat rack-prong; automatic up-down lid on windowseat; pop-out drawer in sideboard; hinged (and lightweight,
  for Mavis's sake) portrait on wall

Sound Effects
  Phone; Doorbell; loud Thumps for tumbles down regular
  and secret staircases to cellar, followed by loud Crash;
  investigative Taps and Thumps by Abel in cellar; loud
  metallic/glass Crash of silver service from kitchen; Barry's
  Footsteps approaching from upstairs area; shrill Screech as

nails are pulled out of rack in cellar; very hollow Boom of wine rack door in cellar; very hollow and ever-louder Footfalls coming up cellar stairs; Slam of kitchen door when Barry/Lottie exit; knocking Thumps from within windowseat before Edgar emerges; Crash in kitchen when Barry/Lottie exit there on bicycle

Costumes/Makeup

Constable's uniform (with helmet, if possible) for Abel; striking smoking jacket for Edgar; silvery gray wig and mustache for Edgar

Note on Set

If stage area is small, eliminate dining table and chairs, and play tea scene on sofa and coffeetable; the "cavalry"-charge scene can also be simplified by having Barry and Lottie merely gallop on foot through front door and then vanish—still with a Crash—into the kitchen, if there is insufficient offstage space to utilize the bicycle.

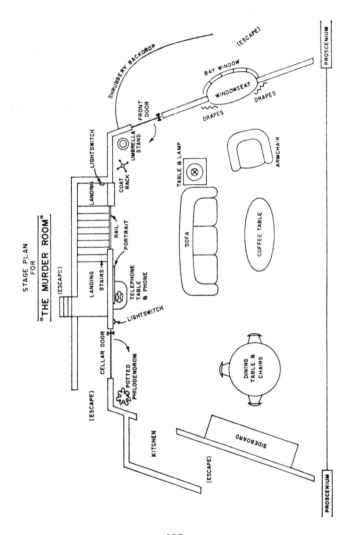

STAGE PLAN
FOR
"THE MURDER ROOM"

108

TREASURE ISLAND
Ken Ludwig

All Groups / Adventure / 10m, 1f (doubling) / Areas
Based on the masterful adventure novel by Robert Louis Stevenson, *Treasure Island* is a stunning yarn of piracy on the tropical seas. It begins at an inn on the Devon coast of England in 1775 and quickly becomes an unforgettable tale of treachery and mayhem featuring a host of legendary swashbucklers including the dangerous Billy Bones (played unforgettably in the movies by Lionel Barrymore), the sinister two-timing Israel Hands, the brassy woman pirate Anne Bonney, and the hideous form of evil incarnate, Blind Pew. At the center of it all are Jim Hawkins, a 14-year-old boy who longs for adventure, and the infamous Long John Silver, who is a complex study of good and evil, perhaps the most famous hero-villain of all time. Silver is an unscrupulous buccaneer-rogue whose greedy quest for gold, coupled with his affection for Jim, cannot help but win the heart of every soul who has ever longed for romance, treasure and adventure.

NO SEX PLEASE, WE'RE BRITISH
Anthony Marriott and Alistair Foot

Farce / 7 m., 3 f. / Int.

A young bride who lives above a bank with her husband who is the assistant manager, innocently sends a mail order off for some Scandinavian glassware. What comes is Scandinavian pornography. The plot revolves around what is to be done with the veritable floods of pornography, photographs, books, films and eventually girls that threaten to engulf this happy couple. The matter is considerably complicated by the man's mother, his boss, a visiting bank inspector, a police superintendent and a muddled friend who does everything wrong in his reluctant efforts to set everything right, all of which works up to a hilarious ending of closed or slamming doors. This farce ran in London over eight years and also delighted Broadway audiences.

"Titillating and topical."
- "NBC TV"

"A really funny Broadway show."
- "ABC TV"

THE OFFICE PLAYS
Two full length plays by Adam Bock

THE RECEPTIONIST
Comedy / 2m., 2f. Interior

At the start of a typical day in the Northeast Office, Beverly deals effortlessly with ringing phones and her colleague's romantic troubles. But the appearance of a charming rep from the Central Office disrupts the friendly routine. And as the true nature of the company's business becomes apparent, The Receptionist raises disquieting, provocative questions about the consequences of complicity with evil.

"...Mr. Bock's poisoned Post-it note of a play."
- New York Times

"Bock's intense initial focus on the routine goes to the heart of *The Receptionist's* pointed, painfully timely allegory... elliptical, provocative play..."
- Time Out New York

THE THUGS
Comedy / 2m, 6f / Interior

The Obie Award winning dark comedy about work, thunder and the mysterious things that are happening on the 9th floor of a big law firm. When a group of temps try to discover the secrets that lurk in the hidden crevices of their workplace, they realize they would rather believe in gossip and rumors than face dangerous realities.

"Bock starts you off giggling, but leaves you with a chill."
- Time Out New York

"... a delightfully paranoid little nightmare that is both more chillingly realistic and pointedly absurd than anything John Grisham ever dreamed up."
- New York Times

SAMUELFRENCH.COM